PRAISE FOR ELYSE FRIEDMAN AND *LONG STORY SHORT*

"Elyse Friedman, author of the story collection *Long Story Short,* might indeed be Toronto's version of France's Michel Houellebecq . . . Friedman, like Houellebecq, is an essential voice." — *Globe and Mail*

"Intensely readable, hilarious, perverse, and never less than The Novel." — *National Post*

"A Friedman story is like an indoor pool with the thermostat set to 86 degrees. It's easy to slip right in." — *Montreal Gazette*

"Fantastic, strange, and moving . . . Highly recommended."
— *Fast Forward Weekly*

"*Long Story Short* spans a broad emotional range, from hilarity to heartbreak, with a dark comedic edge . . . to expose and explore human desires, secrets, and fears, while writing with a sharply observed wit, clever and startling enough to make you laugh aloud. . . . Friedman's surprising revelations always feel earned, never manipulative or gimmicky. . . . Black humour and sharp dialogue are her strengths; she achieves a perfect balance of laughs and pathos . . . A viciously funny and emotionally rewarding read." — *Women's Post*

"Smart, dark, and funny." — *Eye Weekly*

LONG

a novella and stories by

STORY

ELYSE FRIEDMAN

SHORT

ANANSI

First published in hardcover in 2007 by House of Anansi Press Inc.

This edition published in 2008 by
House of Anansi Press Inc.
110 Spadina Avenue, Suite 801
Toronto, ON, M5V 2K4
Tel. 416-363-4343
Fax 416-363-1017
www.anansi.ca

Distributed in Canada by
HarperCollins Canada Ltd.
1995 Markham Road
Scarborough, ON, M1B 5M8
Toll free tel. 1-800-387-0117

House of Anansi Press is committed to protecting our natural
environment. As part of our efforts, this book is printed on paper that
contains 100% post-consumer recycled fibres, is acid-free, and is
processed chlorine-free.

12 11 10 09 08   1 2 3 4 5

LIBRARY AND ARCHIVES CANADA CATALOGUING IN PUBLICATION

Friedman, Elyse, 1963–
Long story short : a novella and stories / Elyse Friedman.

ISBN 978-0-88784-219-1 (bound).— ISBN 978-0-88784-803-2 (pbk.)
I. Title.
PS8561.R4924L66 2007   C813'.54   C2007-903127-7

Jacket design and illustration: Ingrid Paulson
Interior design and typesetting: Ingrid Paulson

Canada Council   Conseil des Arts
for the Arts   du Canada

ONTARIO ARTS COUNCIL
CONSEIL DES ARTS DE L'ONTARIO

*We acknowledge for their financial support of our publishing program
the Canada Council for the Arts, the Ontario Arts Council, and the Government of
Canada through the Book Publishing Industry Development Program (BPIDP).*

Printed and bound in Canada.

For M.A.F-C. With love.

CONTENTS

part one: the novella

        A BRIGHT TRAGIC THING | I

part two: the stories

        THE SOOTHER | 107

        WONDERFUL | 135

        TRUTH | 157

        LOST KITTEN | 175

        THE VIRTUAL TOUR | 199

part one: the novella

A BRIGHT TRAGIC THING

THEY HAD *The Partridge Family, The Brady Bunch,* the crew of *The Love Boat.* They had *Growing Pains, Mr. Belvedere,* and a full set of *Full House.* Todd had a signed Bob Crane that Dave coveted, but he had purchased it on eBay, so it didn't count. Dave had picked up a '76 Farrah Fawcett poster with *Love to Dave* written on it, which was reasonably amusing but, as Todd pointed out, uncountable, since Dave didn't exist in 1976. Farrah had given her love to some other Dave. An old fart by now. They both had Adrienne Barbeau.

The thing began in grade eleven, around the time they started smoking pot. Todd's parents went to see a dinner theatre production of *The Odd Couple* and came home with an eight by ten, black and white photo of Jamie Farr, inscribed with *best wishes for Todd.* Dave thought it was the funniest thing he had ever seen, especially after Todd scanned it and had it printed on matching T-shirts. They wore the shirts to school every Monday—*Jamie-Monday,* they called it—and persisted even after Michael Elliot called them fags, and threatened to beat the crap out of them if they ever wore "that shit" again.

"Hey, brainiac," Todd had shouted as Michael Elliot hulked off down the hallway. "You think fags would be caught dead wearing oversized Jamie Farr T-shirts? These aren't even a hundred percent cotton, you moron."

Michael Elliot returned to crush Todd's nose in his massive hand. The beaming, blood-stained Jamie Farr was funnier than ever and, according to Todd, totally worth the pain and disgrace.

"Clearly, my Jamie no longer measures up," Dave pronounced gravely, the Monday following the incident.

"Sorry, dude, but I believe you're right." Todd finished the spliff they were sharing and flicked it onto the railroad tracks that ran behind the school. "Your unsullied Klinger is comparatively lacklustre. In short, a bore."

"I'm depressed."

"You should be."

"What do you think, pills or razor blade?"

"It's more efficient to shoot yourself."

"True."

"Why waste good narcotics?"

"You're right. Especially since my father owns several pistols."

"Well there you go. Pistols at dawn."

"I can challenge myself to a duel."

"Here." Todd handed his gloves to Dave, who used them to slap his own face sharply.

Much laughter followed, and they were late again for social studies.

That night, Dave retired his humdrum Klinger and searched the Internet for a suitable replacement. He googled *funny T-shirts* and got 3,480,000 hits—a bounty of ostensibly amusing slogan-wear, but several hours of dedicated surfing inspired nary a smirk. Dave had expected a load of so-bad-they're-good choices, but by the time he dropped into bed at 2:15 a.m. he had managed to find only a handful of shirts that were genuinely unintentionally amusing. There was the repulsive *Confucius say, man with hand in pocket feel cocky all day* tee complete with racist cartoon of a "Chinaman" sporting coolie hat and overbite, the egregiously inane *Practise Safe Lunch: Use a Condiment* shirt, and the text-only *Who Needs Big Tits When You Have An Ass Like This?* tee, which he came precariously close to ordering, hesitating just in time to realize that all subtlety would be lost on his classmates, who would assume he was laughing *with* the shirt instead of at it. Dave decided he would have to make his own Jamie-Monday replacement duds. He would contact a list of has-been sitcom stars, solicit autographed photos, and try to one-up Todd on the personalized inscription.

Three weeks later, Dave arrived at school with Betty White's airbrushed visage big across his chest, the following handwritten message partially obscuring her teeth:

> *Dear Dave Burke, Cancer can be beaten! With prayers and best wishes, your friend, Betty.*

"Dude, that's spectacular. How'd you manage it?" Todd shook Pop Rocks into his mouth and chased them with a swig of Red Bull.

"Easy, T. I simply dashed off a note to Ms. White informing her of my failing health and my final wish. I waited a couple of weeks and presto: Betty-Monday."

"Nice."

"Thanks." Dave tried not to crack a smile. "There are others too."

"Others?"

"Other letters. Other shirts."

Todd searched his friend's face. "Oh my god, you can hardly wait till next Monday."

"It's true." Dave laughed against his will.

And the game was on.

Todd and Dave spent all their free time together smoking dope and watching old TV shows, and most of their free time apart researching and contacting washed-up celebrities. Initially they went for the recognizable stars—the Gabe Kaplans, the William Shatners, the Ricardo Montalbans—and succeeded in amassing a sizable collection, but they realized after some time that the sidekick has-beens were infinitely more amusing, and therefore more valuable, than the headliners. Donny Most (Ralph Malph) was better than Henry Winkler (The Fonz). Pat Harrington (Schneider) beat Valerie Bertinelli (Barbara Cooper). Marc Price (Skippy Handleman) was ultimately superior to Michael J. Fox (Alex P. Keaton). So it was that Dave, near the end of grade twelve, came to write to Murray Mortenson, better known as Billy "AWOL" Jones from *Mother Knows Better*. Murray/AWOL appeared on every second or third episode, playing the wiseacre pizza delivery boy who always got the order wrong, and usually arrived late (with an hilarious excuse for his tardiness). The show was a big hit in the early 1980s, but remained on the air for only two years due to a salary dispute involving child actor Tracy Benson, instigated by her megalomaniacal, frequently ravening father/manager. With her waist-length blonde hair, violet eyes, and prominent breast buds, twelve-year-old Tracy was undeniably the draw on *Mother Knows Better*, despite the fact that she was surrounded by a cast of eight, and the mother in question was Julie Magnus, former toast of Broadway and winner of five Tony Awards. The producers tried to replace Tracy with another pubescent Barbie-in-the-making, but the viewers wouldn't have it. Only three episodes of the third season were ever broadcast.

There were fan sites on the Internet for every member of the cast of *Mother Knows Better*, with the exception of Murray Mortenson. Dave had to join up for a free two-week trial of Internet Movie Database Pro to learn that Murray was represented by the True Talent Agency in Rochester, New York, and that according to the IMDB, he had done just one acting job since the demise of MKB—a one-off guest spot playing "Chip" in a made-for-TV Columbo movie.

By the time Dave wrote to Murray, he and Todd had retired their celebrity-Monday T-shirts. Not because they enjoyed the joke any less, but because the apparel seemed to be leading to a vast absence of female attention.

"It's the only reason we're not getting laid," Todd insisted, after the object of his affection, the quirky and alternative Helen Korakianitis, rolled her eyes at his Brice Beckham shirt and told to him to grow-the-fuck-up-already. Dave, who was also into Helen Korakianitis (or "Ghost World," as they called her), concurred, and they began to keep their celebrity cache to themselves. The mania for autographed photos morphed into a quest for signed mementoes—the odder and more personal the better.

May 6, 2007

Murray Mortenson
c/o True Talent Agency
Rochester, New York

Dear Mr. Mortenson,

I'm writing to let you know how much I enjoyed you as Billy "AWOL" Jones on *Mother Knows Better*. I'm sure you get letters like this all the time, but still I feel compelled to tell you that I thought you were the best and funniest thing on a particularly fine and funny show. Why didn't they have you on EVERY episode? They should have!

I know the term 'genius' is bandied about so much these days that it tends to lose its potency, but I don't care, I'm going to use it anyway. When you played the part of "AWOL" you displayed a rare comic genius. I realize that it was the show's writers who made you always have the wrong order, and almost always made you late with the pizza, but the way you PLAYED it was hilarious. Your timing was impeccable. That shoulder shrug thing you did, for example, was subtle brilliance. And the long pause after the "Um..." every time someone asked where you had been. Let's just say your delivery was flawless. (Pardon the pun!)

Anyway, I just think you were under-used in the show, and that it was tragic that Tracy Benson screwed it up for everyone. I know it's none of my business, but why didn't you go on to other sitcoms? How is it that such a gifted young man retired from the business so early? Aside from your excellent guest appearance as 'Chip' in the Columbo movie, I don't think I've seen you in anything else. Have you been in anything else? And if not, why continue to hide your considerable talent under a bushel? I guess you're probably just holding out for the right project, probably disgusted by the junk that passes for entertainment in Hollywood these days. I don't blame you. By the way, if you're wondering why I didn't write to you before, it's because I just discovered the show in reruns on a network we have here in Canada, called TVOPOLIS. I'm only seventeen years old, so I couldn't have seen the show when it originally aired (unfortunately!).

Well, I guess I've taken up enough of your time. I just have one small request before I sign off. Don't worry; it's not for an autographed photo. I'm not one of those parasites who collect and sell signed photos. I'm not the kind of person who would try to profit from a celebrity's generosity. But to be honest, I would love to have some little memento of Murray Mortenson/Billy "AWOL" Jones. Perhaps something that nobody else would want so you could be sure I wouldn't try to sell it on the Internet. Maybe an old shoe, or that cracked mug that you've been meaning to throw in the garbage. Just some small item that has the good "Mortenson vibe." And hey, if you wanted to sign it to Dave Burke, that'd be totally amazing (but you don't have to). And don't worry; I wouldn't use it to try to impress my friends. I pretty much don't even have any friends, so you can trust me on that one.

I've enclosed five dollars for postage. If you don't feel like sending anything, just buy yourself a brewski on me.

Cheers, man. You rock!

Audaciously Yours,
Dave Burke

248 Roseman Avenue
Toronto, Ontario
M4R 1E9

THE FIRST CALL came on May 18th at 6:30 p.m. while Dave was having dinner with his parents and his sister, Kate. There was a policy in the Burke household of not answering the phone during a meal, but because it was a long-distance ring and Kate's boyfriend had just moved with his family to Vancouver, she jumped up to get it and was neither stopped nor reprimanded.

"Hello?" Kate's expectant smile vanished in an instant. "Hold on a second." She thrust the handset toward Dave. "It's for you."

"For me?" Dave couldn't think of anyone who would call him long distance.

"Telemarketing," his father sniffed.

"In the other room, please," said his mother.

Dave moved into the family room. "Hello?"

"Is this Dave Burke?"

"Yeah."

"Seventeen-year-old Dave Burke?"

"Who wants to know?"

"Um…"

"Hello?

"Howdy."

"Who is this?"

"Um…" Silence.

"You're not funny, OK." Dave pressed the "end" button. He checked the call display: *Private Number*. Dave tossed the cordless on the couch and returned to the kitchen.

"Who was it?" his mother asked.

"Prank," he said, forking some penne into his mouth.

"No answering the phone during meals," said his father.

DAVE WAS IN the shower when the second call arrived just after nine o' clock that night. There was a pink Post-it note stuck to his computer screen. The handwritten scrawl said: *Murray Morganson called.* Dave knocked on his sister's bedroom door.

"Can I come in?"

"I'm busy."

"Just for a sec."

"Uch! What?"

Kate was upside down. Dave tried not to look at her ass, which was cute in lululemon yoga pants and had no business being attached to his sister.

"You took this?" Dave waved the Post-it.

"Yeah."

"When did he call?"

"About ten minutes ago."

"He didn't leave a number?"

"I asked, but he said he'd call back."

"Hmm. What did he sound like?"

"I dunno. Like some guy. Why, who is he?"

"Did it sound like Todd at all?"

"No. And anyway it was a long-distance ring."

"Hmm."

"Who is this guy?"

"Nobody, don't worry about it."

"I can just google him, you know." Kate flipped upright as Dave closed the door. "Must be your gay lover," she called out after him.

SUDDENLY THE "UMM…" made sense. That was Billy "AWOL" Jones's signature line when he showed up late with the pizza, and someone asked where he had been or why it had taken so long. But wasn't it a bit weird for Murray Mortenson to call up completely out of the blue and expect him to make that connection? It was weird enough that he had called at all. Dave was reasonably certain he hadn't put a phone number

on his letter, which meant that Mortenson must have con-
tacted Toronto directory assistance to find it. Why would he
do that? What could he possibly have to say to "seventeen-
year-old Dave Burke," as he had put it? Again, Dave considered
the possibility that Todd was fucking with his head. Again,
he concluded that it was unlikely, since they never divulged
which celebs they had written to. Unless Todd had hacked
into his computer—extremely doubtful —he wouldn't have
known about his attempt to contact Murray Mortenson and
therefore wouldn't be impersonating him. And then there
was the matter of the long-distance rings. Dave laughed as he
pondered the notion that he had hung up on a sitcom star—
a has-been, yes, but someone who at some point in his life
had appeared airbrushed on the cover of *Tiger Beat*. Dave did
the math. Murray Mortenson had played an eighteen-year-
old in 1982. That meant he was at least forty now, probably
even older. Was he one of those ancient gay guys, looking for
a teenager to seduce? Toronto wasn't that far to go from
Rochester. Hell, some old farts flew all the way to Bangkok to
get their rocks off. Dave, whose short-term memory wasn't
the greatest, pulled up the missive he'd sent to Murray
Mortenson. Had he included his phone number? No. A cur-
sory glance revealed only name and address. Had he in any
way suggested that he might be a lovesick groupie looking to
hook up? No. But as Dave reread the letter, he realized that
not only had he laid the adulation on a bit thick, he had also
made himself sound like a huge loser. The line about him
pretty much having no friends was especially pathetic. Murray
Mortenson was probably just a soft-hearted guy taking pity

on the dweeb from Canada. Or maybe he thought Dave was some kind of Columbine-in-the-making and that a friendly phone call might help turn him around. Who else but a psycho would be a rabid Billy "AWOL" Jones fan in 2007? Dave smiled. It was too weird that Murray Mortenson had actually phoned him. Todd would laugh his ass off when he found out. Of course, he couldn't tell Todd about it. Not yet. Not until he had something more substantially amusing to relate or display. He felt a small tingle of excitement. He sensed opportunity.

Dave threw off his bathrobe and put on a pair of boxer shorts. He flopped onto his bed and mulled over how he could go about recording the conversation if Murray Mortenson tried to reach him again. He seemed to remember seeing an old mini-cassette recorder somewhere around the house. Maybe in the kitchen junk drawer? Or in the basement with all the tools and picture wire? He wondered if the thing still worked, and if Mortenson would bother calling back. Doubtful. But he would dig out the tape recorder after school tomorrow just in case.

THE NEXT MORNING, Dave was jerking off, mostly to Helen Korakianitis, when the third phone call came. It was 8:18 a.m. There was no landline in Dave's room, so he didn't hear the ring. His mother knocked on his door.

"Dave?"

Fuck. "Just a minute." He was so close, and now the biggest erection-killer in the world was audible and looming. He pulled the duvet over himself.

"There's a call for you. Are you decent?"

Dave adjusted the covers. "Yeah."

His mother entered with the phone. "You're still in bed?"

"I'll be ready."

"You'd better hurry if you want a ride. I'm leaving in ten minutes." She tossed the handset on the duvet and left the room.

Dave knew who was on the phone. Nobody ever called him before school. Not even Todd.

"Hello?"

"Hey, Dave. This is Murray Mortenson calling." The voice was big and smooth and friendly. Announcer voice.

"Oh wow. Hi!"

"How's it going?"

"Good. Pretty good…" Dave thought about the tape recorder that might be in the kitchen drawer. He pulled on a pair of jeans. "How's it going with you?"

"Well, you know, I can't complain."

"Cool," Dave said as he ran down the hall.

"This isn't a bad time to call, is it?"

"No. It's fine." He did the three landing stairs in one jump and hopped the last four of the main staircase. "Just getting ready for school."

"Was that your mom giving you a hard time?"

"Yeah. I grab a ride when it's raining, and she gets all freaked out if I'm, like, ten seconds late."

"So it's raining up there in Toronto, Canada."

"Yeah." Dave moved into the kitchen, fast past his mom who was having coffee at the table.

"It's nice and sunny here in Rochester."

"That's cool."

"You know, my mom was born in Canada."

"Oh really?" Dave rifled through the large drawer next to the dishwasher.

"What are you doing?" said his mother. "Don't you want a ride?"

"Is that her again?"

"Yeah. One sec." Dave put his hand over the mouthpiece. *"I'm on the phone."*

"Fine. But are you coming with or not?"

Dave looked out the window. It was really pissing. Again. It had been an unusually hot spring, with early smog alerts and many short but heavy bursts of humidity-busting rainfall. He looked in the drawer: Scotch tape, birthday candles, food-stained takeout menus, a puffed-out champagne cork, many dried-up pens, a large tangle of string and twist ties, an expired Metropass, a plastic digital watch, a pair of dusty wax lips, one miniature Sony cassette tape, but no mini-recorder. Dave closed the drawer.

"I'll be right down," he said to his mother. "Wait for me, OK?" His mother scowled, but her eyes were smiling—it was the "you're incorrigible" look—which meant she would wait if he hustled.

"Sorry about that," he said into the phone.

"Parents, huh? You can't live with 'em, and you can't kill 'em." Murray Mortenson laughed.

Dave forced a chuckle as he vaulted up the stairs. "Yeah, exactly."

"No, I'm just joshing. Your mom sounds like a very nice lady."

"She's okay. But, um, she's gonna take off without me if I'm not ready in, like, five minutes. And I haven't even brushed my teeth yet."

"Oh. Okay. Go ahead. I wouldn't want you to get rained on."

Was Mortenson being sarcastic? Dave wasn't sure. He said it sincerely, but the announcer voice gave it a sheen of snide.

"I just wanted to thank you for your letter anyway. I figured I'd try to catch you before school. Bad timing, I guess."

"Um, would it be at all possible to call you back? I mean, if you can spare a few minutes, I'd really love to talk a bit. As you know, I'm a huge fan." Dave found a shirt that passed the sniff test, put it on, and buttoned it quickly.

"Well, I usually don't give out my home number—"

"Yeah, I guess. You'd have fans calling you all the time. Um, well maybe you could you call me back? Like after school, or later tonight?"

"What time do you get home?"

Dave tried to figure out how long it would take to walk home, find the tape recorder, and get the thing up and running. "Assuming no detentions, I could be home by four-fifteen-ish. Four-thirty at the latest."

Mortenson chuckled. "All right then. You keep out of trouble, and I'll give you a call at four-thirty—schedule permitting."

"Great. I'll give you my cell number so you can get me directly."

"Super. Shoot."

"It's 416-858-5623."

"DAVID," his mother shouted from downstairs.

"Shit, I gotta go. Sorry."

"I'M LEAVING IN TWO MINUTES."

"No worries, dude. We'll talk later."

"OK. Later, man."

"Sayonara!"

Sayonara was the way Billy "AWOL" Jones signed off whenever he left the gang on *Mother Knows Better*.

"Um, yeah," said Dave. "Sayonara."

DAVE WAS MULLING over matters related to Murray Mortenson when Mrs. Applebaum called on him to comment on Shakespeare's Sonnet 29.

"Mr. Burke?"

"Yes?" The classroom shifted into focus: many people looking in his direction, including Helen Korakianitis one row up and three seats over; Mrs. Applebaum's wry smile because she had caught him napping.

"You've been awfully quiet today. What do you think?"

Luckily, he had been paying enough attention to have the handout open at the correct page. He started to speed-read the poem in front of him. *When, in disgrace with Fortune and men's eyes, I all alone beweep my outcast state*—"About which part specifically?"—*And trouble deaf heaven with my bootless cries.*

"The part we were just discussing."

"Um…" *And look upon myself, and curse my fate.*

"The second quatrain."

"Oh." Dave counted down four lines and began to read aloud. "'Wishing me like to one more rich in hope,' um…he wishes he felt more hope?"

"Yes, we've established that."

Dave mock-sighed and said, "I think I can relate." Everyone laughed, including Mrs. Applebaum. He could usually get away with shit by cracking a joke. Bolstered, he continued with a hint of vocal flourish. "'Featured like him, like him with friends possessed, / Desiring this man's art and that man's scope,' um, he's jealous of one guy's ability…and the other guy's mouth-wash." A few people laughed again, but Helen Korakianitis groaned, and Mrs. Applebaum folded her arms across her chest.

"Look, I know it's the end of the year, people, and it already feels like summer out there, but we still have a bunch of classes left, OK? And guess what? You're still being marked."

Dave tried to stop smiling. He stared at the floor.

"Next week, another short test, then we'll be looking at the excerpt from *Hero and Leander* by Christopher Marlowe." Mrs. Applebaum glanced at the clock. It was 11:59 a.m. People stood up to gather their things. "Please read the poem and be prepared to comment on it."

As Dave was shuffling out of the classroom, Mrs. Applebaum looked askance at him.

"Sorry, about that," he said with a smirk.

"If you want to salvage the A-minus I was prepared to give you, you can hand in a two-page analysis of Sonnet 29 before the end of the year."

"What, just me?"

"You don't have to. In fact, you can dial it in for the rest of the year and settle for a B-minus, if you like. Your choice."

"Two *double-spaced* pages, right?"

Mrs. Applebaum smiled. "You're going on to university, I assume."

"If they'll have me. That's the plan."

"Two pages double-spaced will be fine."

LUNCHTIME. The rain had stopped, and it was muggy and hot all over again.

"Here comes Ghost World," said Todd, quickly wiping his face with a stack of serviettes.

Dave turned and saw Helen Korakianitis slouching toward them through the parking lot, cigarette in one hand, carrot stick in the other. Her fingernails were black. Her boots were big. Dave still had a few fries left, but he pushed his tray away. He took a sip of Sprite and swished it around his mouth, sucking it through the front teeth to clean them.

"How can you guys eat this crap?" Helen said. "Haven't you seen *Super Size Me?*"

"Yes, I know. It's poison and horrible, and my liver is putrefying al—" As Todd spoke, a fast burp erupted suddenly from his throat. "You see!" He looked surprised and embarrassed, but covered by pressing his hand coyly to his chest and fanning himself like a Southern belle. "Oh my heavens, I do believe I've developed a case of the vapours."

Deadpan Helen smiled her small smile. "Seriously, though. It's not just about *your* health and well being, it's about the well being of the rainforests and—"

"I know, I know. I've read *Fast Food Nation,* and I totally agree that taking this repast is cause for reproach. But, Helen, sometimes I get so"—Todd squirmed in his seat—"*hungry.* And the only thing that will satisfy is a big squirt of special sauce. Can you relate?"

Dave laughed but shook his head in disapproval.

"God. Why do I consort with such dweebs?" said Helen, flicking her cig at the giant fibreglass Mayor McCheese at the edge of the patio. It bounced off his mayoral sash and landed in a planter. Dave watched it burn a hole in a red begonia.

"Because we adore you. Right, Dave?"

"But of course…" Dave could feel himself blushing. He stood and carried his tray to the garbage can. "We worship the ground your Blundstones tread upon."

"Uh huh. Right." Helen chomped her carrot and rolled her eyes but did not seem displeased. "Well, in that case, I suppose I'll invite you guys to come swimming at my place after school."

"Fuck off! You have a pool?!"

"No. I'm inviting you to come swim in the laundry sink."

"Holy shit," said Todd. "If I knew you had a pool, I would have been way nicer to you last summer."

"Yeah well, it wouldn't have done you any good. George just put it in last fall." Helen always referred to her father by his first name. Her mother's name was Uranus. She referred to her as "mom." "And George just finished decorating it a couple days ago."

"Streamers and balloons?"

"No. Endless amounts of columns and statuary, and an elaborate waterfall with a Venus de Milo centrepiece. You kind of have to see it to believe it."

"I can't wait. It sounds absolutely smashing." Todd dumped his tray, and the three began the short trek back to school. "You shouldn't be ashamed of your heritage, Helen."

"I'm not. I think the Parthenon is a wonder of architectural balance and harmony. I just don't think the Tiny Town version belongs in my swimming pool in North Toronto."

"We'll be the judge of that. Right, Dave-o?"

"Um, right." Dave had been mulling it over and had just decided that it was more important to see Helen wet in a bathing suit—and to not leave her alone with Todd under those conditions—than it was to stay home and record his prearranged phone call from Murray Mortenson. He realized there was no way Mortenson would call back or send him anything after that, but so be it. A few days earlier, Dave had received a hair scrunchy from Kim Fields, who played Tootie on *The Facts of Life*, autographed with her catchphrase "We are in *trou-ble!*" It would have to do for now. "So should we just get our suits and come right over?"

"Yeah. The sooner the better, 'cause we eat at six, so you'll have to split by a quarter-to or George will get ornery."

"We wouldn't want that."

"And my parents don't know I smoke, so if they come out don't say anything."

"Our lips are sealed."

"I hope they do come out," said Todd.

"Why do you hope that?" said Helen.

"Because." He pinched the small flap of skin on her left elbow. "Dave has always wanted to see Uranus."

Helen yanked her arm away and tried to slap Todd, but he deked out of the way.

"In fact, he told me he'd like to get to know Uranus intimately!"

Helen caught Todd and smacked him repeatedly on the side of the head, which only made him laugh harder.

Dave laughed too.

THE SWIM AT HELEN'S was fun but a little disappointing. Dave had envisioned a small white bikini, one that became transparent when saturated, but Helen had opted for a vintage bathing costume from the 1920s. It was nifty-looking— especially with Helen's bobbed hair—but it was a one-piece that pretty much went from throat to mid-thigh. And it was made of wool. Thick wool. Opaque wool. Dave wasn't complaining though. It was a lot more revealing than Helen's usual ensemble: oversized man's dress shirt with baggy jeans, or a pleated plaid skirt, thick tights, and Blundstones. The flapper swimsuit had allowed him, at least and at last, to form a reasonably clear picture of Helen's contours. Now he could extrapolate.

As if sensing Dave's ardour, Helen's father appeared outside every fifteen minutes or so to check on his daughter. At five-thirty, he started the barbecue and told the boys to clear the pool. Todd tried to suck up and score a dinner invitation— complimenting him on the wonderful landscaping, telling him how much he'd like to visit Greece someday, even inquiring after his marinade recipe—but no sale. George put the meat on the grill and sent the boys out the door. As they were leaving the Korakianitis household, Dave turned on his cellphone and checked the call display to see if Murray Mortenson had phoned at the agreed-upon time. Apparently he had. There was a listing from a Private Caller at 4:31. And another at 4:45. Another at 5:03. And still another at 5:44.

"Hey, you wanna get some Burger Shack?" Todd hung his damp towel around his neck and unlocked his bike.

"Um, nah. I should probably head home."

"Come on. You can jerk off after onion rings. And you won't even need lube."

Dave laughed. He was, in fact, looking forward to a leisurely pre-dinner wank. But he was also famished, and Burger Shack made a good ring. "All right, just let me check these." He entered the code to listen to the four voice messages. The first one was friendly and warm. The big announcer voice said: *"Hey, Dave, Murray Mortenson here. It's four-thirty and I'm calling you back, as discussed. Well, guess I'll try you again in a few minutes. OK. Looking forward to a nice chat."* The next one was cooler but still amiable. *"Hey, Dave. Murray Mortenson here. Well, it looks like you've been delayed, or maybe you got that detention after all. Heh, heh, I hope not. All right… You take care now. Buh-bye."* Dave thought he could detect a hint of peevishness in the "buh-bye," but he wasn't certain. The third call was simply a hang up. The last one, the 5:44 call that Dave had missed by only a minute or two, was surprisingly nasty. *"Well, Dave, I guess you're just a fuck-up. And guess what? I don't have time for fuck-ups. Sayonara, jerk."* Click.

"What?"

"Holy shit!"

"What the hell is so funny?"

Dave pocketed his cellphone and got on his bike. "I'll tell you when we get to Burger Shack."

AFTER ONION RINGS, and then dinner at Todd's parents, Dave and Todd retired to The Lair to transfer Murray Mortenson's phone messages onto CD. The Lair was Todd's rec room, which he had recently been allowed to take over as his bedroom. It was perfect—big, out of parental earshot, and easy to sneak in and out of due to a window in the corner that his parents believed to be painted shut, but that Todd had patiently freed with an exacto knife over a period of three weeks. Everything in the basement that used to gall and embarrass now amused him immensely—the cheap wood panelling, the golf-themed decorations, the teardrop-shaped bean-bag loungers that looked like vinyl manatees splayed across the carpeting, and the *pièce de résistance*: the faux-oak wet bar in the corner (stripped of booze, alas, except for a decorative bottle of gin-seng liqueur with a human-looking ginseng root floating in the amber liquid). Hanging in the centre of the room above the fake fireplace was a ten-point buck trophy-head made out of fibreglass. From the antlers of the buck, Todd had dangled some of his prized celeb scores—one of Connie Needham's vintage toe-socks, a signed coffee mug complete with genuine lipstick smear from Gabrielle Carteris, and his most recent acquisition—a broken blow-dryer, autographed by Jason Hervey, who played Fred Savage's older brother, Wayne, on *The Wonder Years*.

None of these treasures compared, however, to the hilariousness of being called a fuck-up by Billy "AWOL" Jones. Todd was impressed. It was his idea to save the audio on CD. At first the boys tried connecting the phone directly to the PC—for optimum transfer quality—but they couldn't figure out how to upload anything but text messages. In the end, they simply played the voice messages from the cell directly into the PC's microphone and then burned them onto a disc. Todd was eager to find a picture of Murray Mortenson to create a handsome "Sayonara, Jerk!" CD cover in Photoshop, but it was getting late, and Dave was bagged from swimming and sunshine and too much food, so they decided to do it another day.

Call number eight arrived several hours later at 11:54 p.m. Dave had been asleep a short time when the cellphone on the night table woke him. He wasn't used to his new personalized ringtone—a man burping the opening bars of O Canada!—so though his body went through the automatic motions of answering the telephone, he was quite disoriented when he said hello, and heard: "Hey, Dave. Murray Mortenson here."

"Oh...um, hi."

"I didn't wake you, did I?"

"Um...I was sort of drifting off."

"Aw jeez, sorry man. Fuck!"

"No, it's all right."

"And you got school tomorrow..."

"It's OK. Don't worry about it." Dave thought Murray Mortenson sounded drunk. There was music playing in the background. He tried to place it.

"I just been feeling shitty about that message I left ya."

"Oh. Yeah."

"Did you get that message?"

"Yeah. I got it." Dave recognized the song in the background. It was a weird, faster version of the Gary Jules song—"Mad World"—from the *Donny Darko* movie.

"It was just wrong of me to label you a fuck-up before I knew what the deal was, you know what I'm saying?"

"Yeah." Dave heard Murray take a sip from a bottle; there was that suction pop when lips leave glass at the end of a hit.

"I mean, for all I know someone stole your cellphone, or you were hit by a car or something. Abducted by aliens, kidnapped by insurgents." Murray laughed loud.

"Yeah."

"So what's the deal, dude? Everything okey-doke or what?

"My grandmother had a heart attack."

"Aw shit. You see, I knew it! Fuck me!"

As soon as the excuse flew out of his mouth Dave felt a small jab of guilt. This was followed by a wave of laughter that he suppressed by burying his face in the pillow.

"Wow, man…I'm sorry! Is she—did she make it?"

Dave tried not to think about his Grandma Rose, who had, in fact, died of a heart attack two years ago. He had to choke back his laughter before he could murmur, "Yeah. She made it."

Mortenson misinterpreted the pause and the tightness of Dave's speech. "Listen, man, it's tough when shit like this goes down. It's all right to cry if you want."

Cry? Why would he cry over something non-existent disappearing? You don't cry over zero minus zero. Ever since

Dave was a small child, his Grandma Rose had been suc-
cumbing to the erasing effects of early-onset Alzheimer's. By
the time he was old enough to remember her, she was inani-
mate, a hull that sat in their house, facing the window or the
television—more sculpture than human—dozing in sweat-
ers too warm for the weather. Grandma Rose had never
inspired tears from Dave. Laughter? Yes. She definitely made
him laugh. Like when she would suddenly pass gas in the
middle of a meal, or when a synapsis would mysteriously
succeed in firing, and she would blurt out a non sequitur:
"Because the dog was on the chesterfield!" Or when he would
discover one of her crazy stashes, i.e., an old chicken bone
wrapped in toilet paper, folded into a dish towel, and then
hidden away in one of his running shoes. She made him laugh
when she wandered out of the house one day and was found
later by the police in the ravine around Yonge and St. Clair,
eating pebbles and all covered in burrs. And she was still
making him laugh now, on the phone with Murray Mortenson, as the grandma excuse flew out of his mouth and he
recalled a mandatory—now legendary—visit he and Todd
had made to Grandma Rose in the nursing home a couple of
months before her death. Dave had been addressing her in
the usual fashion—*Hi, Grandma, how are you feeling today? Are
you feeling OK? It's pretty warm in here. Do you want me to open the
window? I think I'm going to open the window, OK?*—until Todd
pointed out that it didn't much matter what he said, since she
didn't understand a word anyway. Todd proceeded to talk to
Grandma Rose using the same pleasant, inquiring tone as
Dave, but he was saying things like: "So, Grandma Rose,

how's your rotten old crotch today? Is it still itchy? Hmm? Is it still stuffed full of sauerkraut and old socks? It is! Oh, that's nice. And tell me, Grandma, is Tim the orderly still dropping by every morning to drink his chai tea out of your ass? He is! Wonderful. He did *what* this afternoon? He tied your tits into a sailor's knot? Oh my goodness, Grandma! Was that before or after you got Polident all over his testicles?"

It was rude and crude, but Dave found it hilarious. It was so funny, in fact, that he had to leave the room and wait for Todd in the visitors' lounge, because he couldn't stop laughing. He laughed so hard and so long, it actually hurt the muscles in his stomach. Even now at the thought of it Dave was finding it difficult to suppress the laugh urge, especially since Mortenson thought he was all choked up.

Finally, he said, "No, I'm all right. Really." He heard Mortenson take another swig of whatever he was drinking.

"So how is she doing? Do the doctors think she's going to come through it OK?"

Dave decided to lighten things up. "For sure. It turns out it was more of an angina thing than a heart attack."

"Oh really?"

"Yeah. I mean, we thought it was a heart attack when we rushed to the hospital this aft—which is why I couldn't take your calls, obviously—but it turned out to be more of an angina thing, so she's going to be fine."

"Well, that's super news."

"Yeah. It's a relief. Anyway, sorry about not being available." Dave realized he had magically come up with the ideal excuse. "I had to turn my cellphone off in the hospital. "

"No worries, dude. I'm just regretful that I called you a fuck-up. I mean, that's a shitty thing to hear from someone you look up to and admire."

"Oh that's OK."

Murray didn't say anything for a few seconds. Dave noticed that the fast version of "Mad World" had ended. A song that sounded familiar—some oldie—was now playing in the background.

"So...that letter you sent me."

"Yeah."

"That was a really great letter, man."

"Oh. Thanks."

"A really great letter. And good timing too."

"Oh yeah?"

"Yeah. Perfect timing. I just really needed something to lift the spirits, so to speak."

"Oh. Well, I'm glad the timing was good."

Mortenson laughed. "You know that thing you said about the shoulder shrug I used to do on the show?"

"Um...I don't remember *exactly*."

"Well, you said something like...um, what was it again? Well hell, hold on a sec, I've got your letter right here. Might as well just read it." There was a short pause while Mortenson located the bit he was looking for. "Oh yeah, here it is, um: *'Your comic timing was impeccable. That shoulder shrug thing you did, for example, was subtle brilliance.'*"

"Oh right. Well, it's true," Dave said, trying to stoke up the bullshit. "That shoulder thing was pretty awesome."

"Thanks, man. You know, I'm not trying to fish for more compliments, I just think it's very cool that you noticed that. I mean, I *created* the shoulder thing. It wasn't in any of the scripts initially."

"Really?"

"Hell, yeah. Remember episode four, the one where Kelli copies Lindsay's homework?"

"Yeah," Dave lied.

"I did it for the first time in that episode. I don't know why exactly; it just felt like I needed to fill the long pause with *something*. It was instinctive, I guess. And then after, it got a huge laugh, Hal told the writers to start writing it into the script."

"Hmm. Cool."

"Hal was really inclusive in that way. He encouraged us to come up with stuff for the show."

"Neat." Dave checked the time. It was after midnight.

"Yeah. Hal was amazing. The best. He was like a dad to me."

"So do you still keep in touch?"

"Oh yeah. I mean, once in a while. Of course, he's super-busy with a lot of projects. And I'm busy. You know…"

"Yeah."

"Plus he's got, like, five kids and a bunch of grandkids. That takes a lot of time and attention." Mortenson went silent for a few seconds, then he cleared his throat and said, "But a lot of actors have little things they do. Little signature moves."

"Oh really."

"Yeah. Like Jessica Lange. She has the pick-the-piece-of-tobacco-off-the-lip-after-taking-the-first-drag-of-a-cigarette thing. You know? It just makes the action seem more true to life. I've seen her do it in, like, three different movies."

"Who's Jessica Lange?"

"Shit, man! One of the hottest actresses ever. Way hotter than Tracy Benson could ever hope to be! Didn't you ever see *The Postman Always Rings Twice* or *Tootsie? King Fuckin' Kong*?"

"Wasn't that Naomi Watts?"

"No, man. I'm talking about the remake, not the remake of the remake."

"I think I remember her from *Tootsie*. She's the blonde, right?"

"Damn right she's the blonde." Mortenson took another swig, then burped. "Pardon my French."

"Hey, what's that song in the background?"

"'World Where You Live.' Crowded House."

"Oh."

"I got the jukebox doing a sweet eighties medley."

"Cool."

"I guess you're pretty young, huh?"

"Well, I'm seventeen."

"Shit. That's how old I was when I got the gig on *Mother Knows Better*."

"Really?"

"I guess it ain't so young." Mortenson laughed. "Hell, I was into all kinds of shit already. Especially after we started getting some recognition."

"I bet."

"I got stories," Mortenson said, ready to launch.

"Shit, man. I'd *really* love to hear them sometime, but—"

"Oh crap! You got school tomorrow."

"Yeah."

"Poor bastard." Mortenson laughed and swigged.

Dave wasn't tired. He was pissed that all the conversational gold was going unrecorded. "So, um, is there anyway I could call you back sometime?"

"Yeah, what the hell...I'll give you my cell number."

Dave scrambled for pen and paper.

"You got a pen?"

"Yeah."

"All right. It's 555-363-7740. Just don't give it to everybody and their goddamn grandma."

"I won't."

"Shit. Sorry, man. Bad choice of words."

"It's OK."

"Send my best to your granny, OK?"

"I will."

"She's gonna be all right."

"I know. Thanks."

"OK, I'll talk to you soon."

"Bye for now."

"Sayonara, man."

OVER THE NEXT two weeks, Murray Mortenson telephoned fifteen times and spoke to Dave on twelve of those occasions (the three times he called during school hours, Dave ignored the urgent vibrating in his shirt pocket). Mostly he called after 11:00 p.m., usually from a bar stool in a lounge called

Philbo's. Dave learned more than he'd ever thought he'd know about Murray Mortenson over the course of those dozen conversations. He learned that his beverage of choice was Budweiser (often chased with a Cutty Sark) and that he drank at Philbo's nearly every night (and not just because it was within walking distance of his one-bedroom condo in the East End district of Rochester). The jukebox at Philbo's was good, and so were the bartenders, especially Kiniesha, who poured generously and had gorgeous brown eyes, so too bad she was married. In 1991, Murray's mom and stepdad moved to Phoenix. He rarely saw them. Ditto his little sister—a nurse—who lived in Yonkers. Nobody knew what happened to his father. He walked out when Murray was six. Christmas gifts arrived by mail for three or four years and then stopped. The man was never heard from again. Murray's mom figured he was dead because he didn't resurface when Murray became famous. Good. Good riddance. The Christmas gifts were lousy, and so were the beatings. Murray can still remember the black leather belt with the silver rivets—the way his father used to snap it. In 1988, Murray married Allison Collins. The union lasted seven and a half months. No children, thank god, just a hamster named Sunny that Mortenson wasn't nuts about at the time, but found himself missing when Allison took him with her. Murray realized the relationship was over when Allison intentionally burned his bicep with the curling iron she used to curl her bangs every morning. That Allison was a hellcat. Then she turned religious. In 1988, she looked like Christina Applegate. The last time he saw her—about six years ago—she had short brown hair and a bit of a moustache. Mortenson would remarry if he could find a special lady. But it hasn't happened yet. He still has a scar on his bicep from the second-degree curling iron burn. It's kind of brown and looks like one of those flattened-out clouds you occasionally see.

Dave also heard a lot about Mortenson's prized possession: a 1968 Camaro z-28, white with black stripes. And that he had sex with Tracy Benson when she was just thirteen years old, in a field full of electrical transmission towers. Murray was seventeen. Tracy was a star.

When Mortenson was drunk, he would talk about the old days. Mortenson talked about the old days a lot. When he was very drunk, Mortenson would talk about having sex with Tracy in the electrical field. Dave had heard about it—and recorded it—three times in just under two weeks. The first time was a throw-away boast—Mortenson bragging about "nailing" Tracy Benson in the electrical field. The second time was a more drawn-out version in which he reviewed—unfavourably for the most part—Tracy's sexual performance and different elements of her anatomy. The third time was truncated, nothing more than a springboard into a venomous rant about Tracy Benson. Todd wanted to try to sell this last version to a tabloid, or at least upload it onto the Internet, but Dave told him to cool his jets and be patient. Plenty more where that came from, since Mortenson was telephoning practically every night. And so they just transferred the recording to CD and listened to it whenever they needed a laugh.

M. MORTENSON RECORDINGS. June 2007. 12:55 a.m. (Mortenson trashes T. Benson)

"... Um, sorry about that. I just had to grab some water."

"I didn't wake you again, did I?"

"It's OK."

"Sorry, man. I just felt like rappin', and I'm sick a talkin' to Leon."

"He's the bartender?"

"No. You're thinking of Lonzell. Leon's a regular. The ex-cop."

"Oh yeah."

"I told you about him, right?"

"A little. He's the guy that got turfed for stealing drugs."

"Right. He didn't do the drugs, he just wanted to make some extra cash. Anyway, he's all bummed 'cause his gal pal dumped him."

"Oh. That's a drag."

"Aw, shit. She dumps him every three months. They'll get back together in a couple weeks once she's had her fun."

"Oh."

"I mean, he's an all-right guy and I feel sorry for him and everything, it's just whenever he's going through this it's all he can talk about. Doesn't wanna hear about anything else, you know what I'm saying?"

"Yeah."

"I mean, if it were for real, fine. I'm happy to listen and be a friend. But it happens all the time... This is, like, the third time in the past year."

"Really?"

"It gets tired, man."

"I guess."

"And the woman ain't even worth it."

"Hmm."

"I know her. I know what she does. She breaks up with him every time she wants to screw someone else. Then, once she's got her rocks off, she goes back to Leon."

"Yikes."

"It's 'cause she doesn't want to cheat. She thinks she's being all ethical or something."

"Weird."

"Yeah. Hang on a sec, OK? Hey, Miranda, set me up again. Hi. Sorry 'bout that. So... speaking of no-good blondes, were you by any chance watching the TV tonight?"

"I watched for a bit, yeah."

"Did you catch you-know-who skating her ass off?"

"Um, no—"

"I couldn't believe it, man. I'm just sittin' at home, surfing around, tryin' to eat my supper, and all of a sudden I see Miss Comeback Kid gettin' tossed in the air by Carl fuckin' Baldwin."

"Who... Tracy Benson?"

"Yeah, Tracy Benson. Who do you think I'm talkin' about? Tatum fucking O'Neal?"

"Sorry. I wasn't—"

"I swear it put me off my food. Couldn't eat the rest of my dinner."

"Yikes."

"You know we went out for a bit."

"Yeah—"

"First time I screwed her was in the middle of an electrical field!"

"Yeah, you told me about tha—"

"Thirteen years old, brother. Her, not me. I was seventeen."

"Wow."

"Fuckin' skank. She dumped my ass a week later."

"Really?"

"Started seeing Donny Matthews. Christ! Remember that doofus?"

"No."

"You don't remember Donny Matthews? Boyz 'n' the Band?"

"Um...?"

"Piece of shit kiddie band that was popular for about five minutes."

"I don't remember."

"Yeah, well, I'm not fuckin' surprised. Anyway, they were hot shit for a while there. Donny was the prettiest of the pretty boyz. You know, curly blond mop-top, non-threatening girly face. Kinda like a young Leonardo DiCaprio with a Harpo wig on. Heh, heh, heh."

"That's funny."

"So Tracy and I are goin' out for about a week, and things are goin' good, you know, gettin' hot and heavy—we were always messing around behind the set and stuff. And then I finally nail her in this electrical field, and three days later she calls it quits on me."

"Oh, for some reason I thought you guys went out longer."

"Good way to give a guy a complex, right? Shit. If it hadn't been for all them Mother Knows Better groupies lining up to nibble my dick, I might a been traumatized or somethin'. Heh, heh, heh..."

"Yikes."

"But still. The bitch didn't even have the decency to tell me. She just shows up two days later in Donny Matthews's stretch limo, and they're all over each other right in front of me like nothin' ever happened between us."

"That sucks."

"Damn right it sucks. You don't a treat a person like that. Especially a fellow castmate. I tell ya, it put me off my dinner when I saw her twirling through the air on Skating with Celebrities. *Jesus, fuck! Skating with Sluts is what they should call it. Heh, heh, heh . . ."*

"That's funny."

"I kept waiting for Carl to drop her on her ass, but it didn't happen, unfortunately."

"Well, you can always tune in next week."

"Yeah, that's true. Heh, heh, heh . . . Hey, Miranda, set me up again. Yeah. You know it sounds retarded, but that show is one mother of a hit."

"I know."

"I caught a couple episodes the first season, and I thought, Shit, I could do that. I mean, I can skate pretty good. I used to play hockey when I was a sprout."

"You should've called them up."

"Well . . . I sorta did. I mean, I called my agent about it."

"Oh yeah?"

"Yeah. Well, that's his job, not mine. I don't know . . . I guess they had enough celebrities for a while. They said they'd let us know. Anyway, fuck that. I'm gonna call Frank tomorrow and tell him to forget about it. Even if they do contact us with an offer, there's no way I'm following Tracy Benson. Even if I can skate a hell of a lot better than that two-timing skank."

"Hmm. Can you dance? Maybe you should try Dancing with Celebrities or Cooking with Celebrities?"

"Nah, I don't dance. Maybe the cooking thing . . . I don't know. Too bad they don't have Drinking with Celebrities. I could be the star of that production, no problem, heh, heh, heh. That's one fuckin' contest I'd win hands down."

"I'd tune in for it."

"Me and Paula Abdul getting hammered here at Philbo's."

"I'd like to see that."

"Me too, brother, me too. Oh well... at least she can't win an Emmy for twirling around in a tiny skating skirt. You know that cow won an Emmy?"

"No, I didn't know th—"

"Can you believe it?! What a joke. Back in 1988. Played some bitch with an eating disorder. Bulimia or some fuckin' thing. Wins herself an Emmy by pretending to make herself barf every five minutes."

"Yikes."

"Some lame-o movie-of-the-week."

"Hmm."

"I thought, I'll stick something down her throat, and you can give me a fuckin' Emmy. Heh, heh, heh."

"That's funny."

"Hey! Here comes my man, Daryl! How's it hanging, big man? Just jawing with my buddy, Dave who lives up in Canada. Yeah. Heh, heh... Blame Canada, man! Hey, Miranda, set us up here, would ya? You want a pitcher? Cool. So, listen, Dave-o, I think I'm gonna split."

"No probs."

"I was just kidding about Canada."

"I know."

"All right. Nice talking to you. I'll talk to you soon, OK?"

"Yup. Talk soon."

"WHAT THE HELL'S the matter with you?" Todd kicked at the worn-out treads on his friend's Pumas. Dave was prostrate on the grass, face down, under a maple tree at the edge of the soccer field.

"He's obviously sleeping," said Helen. "Stop kicking him."

"What the fuck?" Dave rolled over and sat up.

"We were supposed to meet at The Good Bite. Are you drunk or something?"

Dave stood and wiped dust and grass from his jeans. "Shit. I think I fell asleep."

"Up all night whacking your tack again?"

Helen rolled her eyes. "Be more puerile."

"Is that a challenge, Helen? 'Cause you know I can be."

"Please don't."

Dave reached for the can of Coke in Todd's hand. "Give me a sip, asshole."

"Fuck you," said Todd. "I don't want your sleeping-sickness germs. Look at you, you've got grass indentations all over your face."

"I'm not sick. I'm bagged."

"Just give him a sip," said Helen.

Todd obeyed. "Here. Finish it."

As Dave drained the Coke, Helen moved close and picked a tangle of dead grass out of his hair. Dave smiled, his hand automatically brushing the spot where the grass had been.

Todd burped. "So, Helen," he said, knocking the piece of Dave-grass from her fingers. "We have a very important question to ask you."

"Uh huh." She folded her arms across her chest. "And what would that be?"

"Yes, what would that be?" said Dave, crumpling the Coke can against a tree.

"Well, the thing is…" Todd hung his head in a display of mock bashfulness. "We were wondering if you would…Aw, shucks, Helen. Will you go to the prom with us?"

"*Us?*" said Helen with a wry smile. "You're both going to take me to the prom?"

"That's right," said Todd. "And before you answer, I want you to think about that, OK? That's *two* corsages, Helen. One for each wrist. Very flash, not to mention symmetrical."

"Hmm. How tempting." She lit a cigarette, blew smoke. "And I suppose I'll have to kiss you both goodnight?"

"No. Just me," said Todd. "But to be fair, we should probably let Dave watch if we end up making sweet love to each other."

"I wouldn't count on that," said Helen.

"OK. Forget that part. But we should definitely all go to the prom together. Don't you think? I mean, why stop freaking out our classmates now, at this late date?"

Helen laughed.

"So what do you say?"

"Is this for real?" Helen looked at Dave, who had only just heard of the arrangement.

"Um, sure. But do you guys even want to go the prom? I mean, we're not exactly prom types. What are *we* going to do at the prom?"

"Duh," said Todd. "Get fucked up and laugh at all the morons dancing around in their finery. I wouldn't miss it for the world."

"So you're not gonna dance?" asked Helen. "You're just going to stand around laughing at people?"

"No. If you want to dance, I could dance." Todd demon-strated a few moves. "As it happens, I do a fantastic Flintstone Flop."

"Is that right?"

"And Dave's funky chicken is really not to be missed."

Helen smiled at Dave. "Well, in that case, I guess the answer is yes."

"Cool," said Todd. "Let's do it."

"You sure they're still selling tickets?"

"I think so. And even if the official selling period is over, I'm sure if we want to go to our prom, they'll let us buy some freakin' tickets."

"I guess," said Dave. "Well, I'd better get my gown to the cleaners."

"Yeah, especially if it's still covered in vomit," said Todd.

Helen checked her watch. "Oh shit. We're going to be late if we don't hustle." She flicked her cig as they headed across the soccer field to school. "I trust you guys are ready for the test," she said, picking up the pace, big boots moving fast over the green.

"But of course," said Todd.

"What test?" said Dave.

THAT NIGHT DAVE turned off his cellphone at nine o'clock. He was in bed by ten and asleep by ten-thirty. Somewhere around three, he started to have the "can't find a urinal" dream—the one he dreamed repeatedly when he needed to take a piss but was too tired to get conscious and go to it. On this night, the toilets and urinals were overflowing with feces and long loops of crumpled toilet paper, too disgusting to even whiz into. At exactly 4:44 a.m.—Dave stared at the triple red digits on the clock when he awoke—the half gallon of chocolate soy milk he consumed before going to sleep finally roused him and sent him slouching to the bathroom. On his way back to bed he made the mistake of looking at his cellphone. There were four new messages.

"Fucking hell," he muttered, checking the display. Sure enough, it was Murray Mortenson who had phoned each time. The first call was at 10:59. He tried a few minutes later at 11:04, again at 12:30, and most recently at 1:48 a.m. Dave flipped the phone shut and slid it across the bedside table. He tried to go back to sleep. He thought about his world religions test. He was sure he had pretty much flubbed it, probably just barely passed the thing, and it was all Mortenson's fault. If he hadn't been so tired all the time he would've remembered to study. Had he even skimmed the appropriate chapters in the World Religions textbook he would've easily aced the test. But he hadn't remembered to study. He'd been too tired to remember. These days he was either losing quality sleep to take Mortenson's incessant calls, or he was over at Todd's Lair, transferring and cataloguing the Mortenson tapes in the computer. All his free time was being eaten up by the former Billy "AWOL" Jones. It was like having a part-time job—but without pay. Here he was in the last two weeks of school, when his lazy teachers calculated up to half of his overall marks based on tests, and he was screwing up. Todd wasn't screwing up. Todd got to listen to the Mortenson tapes and laugh his ass off. Then Todd got to go study for his exams or write his essays, and hit the hay at a reasonable hour. He didn't have to stay up past midnight practically every night of the week with a tape recorder pressed to the phone, making it difficult to hear half the time, and really uncomfortable to boot, goddammit.

Dave tried to get back to sleep.

He could not get back to sleep.

He decided he may as well get up and study for his upcoming history exam. First, though, he would quickly listen to the messages.

#1) 10:59 p.m.

"Yeah, hey, Dave. Murray Mortenson here. Just thought I'd see if you were around. Um...OK. Sayonara, amigo."

#2) 11:04 p.m.

"Hey, Dave. Me again. I forgot to tell you that my cell is dead. But I'm home, so if you want to call me back you can reach me at 555-454-1720. OK. Give me a call, brother."

Dave noticed that Mortenson was already slurring by the second call. A bad sign.

#3) 12:30 a.m.

"Well, Dave, I guess you're out. Or maybe you're already asleep. Who knows? (sigh) Shit, man. I'm having a bad day...a real bad one. If you get this message, call me at home, OK? Doesn't matter what time. Just call when you get this."

#4) 1:48 a.m.

*"Hey. It's Murray again. Shit, man, I think I did something really fuckin'
stupid. Fuck! Fuck me!* OK. *Call me when you get this. Doesn't matter
what time."*

The last message gave Dave a chill. He had visions of
Mortenson hunched over the defiled corpse of Tracy Benson,
her head bashed in with her own Emmy, her throat slit with
her *Skating with Celebrities* ice skate. He looked at the clock: 5:13
a.m. Dave rummaged in his backpack and fished out a fresh
pack of mini-cassette tapes. He labelled one and inserted it
into the machine. Mortenson picked up after the first ring.

"Hello?"

"Hey, it's Dave."

"Hey! Dave-o! Hold on a sec. Let me turn down the tunes."

Dave listened while Mortenson clattered around. He heard
him knock something over. There was a crash and a curse. Then
the volume of the music went way down, followed by thirty
more seconds of rattling around before Mortenson returned.

"Hey there."

"Are you OK?"

"Well, I'm pretty fuckin' looped if you wanna know the
truth."

"Oh yeah? So what's going on?"

"Just listening to my favourite album of all time: *Non-Stop
Erotic Cabaret*. I tell you, Marc Almond's a fucking genius!"

"No, I mean, *what's going on*? You left me a bunch of messages. I thought something was the matter with you."

"Whoa. Something the matter with *you*, man? You sound all peeved off."

"Yeah, well…I'm tired, OK. It's five o' clock. I should be sleeping. Plus I got shit to do, tests to study for…I thought there was something wrong with you. I mean, you called, like, four times in a row. I figured there was something wrong."

No response.

"Hello?"

Nothing.

"Hello-o? Anybody home?" Dave listened for a few moments to the faint strains of "Tainted Love" playing in the background. Then he heard something odd. He heard what he thought was the sound of Murray Mortenson crying. A tremor of shock wowed through him. Could it be that Mortenson was actually *crying*—or, more accurately, trying in vain to stifle a series of guttural sobs—on tape? Dave pressed the mini-recorder closer to the earpiece.

After a bit, he said: "Hey man. Are you OK?"

"Tainted Love" for a few seconds more and then finally Murray spoke.

"I'm fine," he said, clearing his throat. The announcer sheen returned to his voice. "But you should head to bed. You got school tomorrow, and it's pretty late."

"Well, technically it's pretty early. And I'm pretty much up now. So don't worry about it."

"Oh. I see. Well, sorry. Didn't mean to interfere with your schedule." Mortenson was slurring pretty badly. "Interfere" came out as *inner-fear*.

"I said don't worry about it. It's cool. So what's going on? You said you were having a bad day...that you did something stupid."

"Yeah." Murray sighed deeply. "I had a big fight with my agent."

"Oh." Dave felt disappointed. "Well, that's not so bad, is it?"

"Then I fired his ass. *Fuck!* Fuck me!"

"Well...um, can't you just unfire him?"

"Nah. Not a chance. We said some shit...And anyway he's been really fuckin' useless lately. I mean, did you see that celebrity game show marathon thing the other night?"

"No...I've been pretty busy."

"I couldn't fuckin' believe it! This chick who used to be on *Trading Spaces* was one of the celebrities."

"Who? Paige Davis?"

"You've heard of her? You get that up there?"

"Yeah. She's pretty cute."

"Fine. She's cute. But since when is she an actor? She hasn't even been on that *Trading Spaces* show for, what, the past three years?"

"I don't know."

"No she's been gone for, like, three years. So how is she a celebrity? I mean, Leslie Nielson I can understand. But Paige Davis? Jesus fuck! She's getting hired and I'm not?!"

"Yeah. That's true. That sucks, man."

"Verne Troyer. That midget. He's getting work."

"Oh yeah?"

"Hell, yeah. He did *The Surreal Life*. Didn't you see that?"

"Um, not that season."

"Well he was on one. National frickin' TV. All my agent gets me is voice-overs for local radio ads. But the midget is getting coast-to-coast exposure on *The Surreal Life.*"

"Yeah, but you don't want to be on that show. That's for freaks and burnouts."

"I guess…I don't know."

"*I* know. You're too good for that. You're a great actor."

Mortenson sighed. "Oh come on, man."

"You are. I'm sure one of these days you'll be in the spotlight again."

"You think?"

An image of Todd uploading the Mortenson tapes onto the Net flashed through Dave's head. "For sure."

"Thanks, Dave-o. You're a pal."

Dave felt a shimmer of guilt. He said, "Anyway. Maybe it's good that you fired your agent. Maybe a new guy is what you need to get some stuff going again."

"Yeah. Probably. But it's not that easy."

"Your agent can't be the only guy in town."

"Well…he is, sort of. There are five agencies in Rochester, and I've been with four of 'em."

"What about the fifth?"

"I'm pretty sure it's just for models."

"Oh. Well, there are other towns, right?"

"Yeah. That's true. There are other towns…" Mortenson went silent for a while.

Dave said, "Well, I should probably go study for a bit."

"Oh shit. I keep forgetting about your school."

"Yeah, me too." Dave laughed. "Oh well. Only three more days."

"Then you're done for the summer?"

"Well, three more days of regular school, then prom Saturday, then exams all next week. Then I'm done. Just a bit of graduation stuff after that—rehearsals and whatnot."

"That's great, man."

"Yeah. I'm looking forward to a break."

"I'll have to get you that memento you asked for in your letter. Some kind of graduation present."

"Really? That'd be great. But don't worry about it. You've got enough to worry about right now."

"Hey, no sweat. I think I know just the thing for a diehard Billy "AWOL" Jones fan."

"Well, that'd be awesome. But you don't have to."

"No worries, bro. So, you got yourself a hot date for the prom?"

"Um...I'm sort of going with a couple friends."

"Oh. Well, that's all right. You got some friends to hang out with. I'm sure you'll have a good time." Mortenson didn't sound so sure. He sounded sorry for Dave.

"It should be OK."

"Well, man. I think I'm toast. I should probably go crash."

"All right."

"You take care now."

"You too."

"See you soon."

"Talk soon."

DAVE WENT TO Sam Snyder's on Yonge Street and asked the salesman for the ugliest tux they had.

"Officially, we have no ugly tuxedos," said the salesman, opening a binder full of laminated photos. "But unofficially, I think I have something you might be interested in."

THE JACKET AND PANTS were the colour of orange sherbet. The cummerbund was dark apricot and made of a material that reminded Dave of hotel bedspreads. The shirt had ruffles on ruffles. The bow tie was white and oversized and satin—a clip-on, so Dave had no trouble dressing himself for the big night. He'd rented a pair of white patent leather shoes to go with the outfit, and completed it by pinning a carnation that had been dyed an unnatural blue to his lapel. He looked wonderfully awful.

Todd opted for vintage tails—1930s jacket and pants, paired with a novelty tuxedo T-shirt and red Converse high-tops. When Helen saw them coming up the walk to her house, she snipped: "Well, if it isn't Sammy Maudlin and Captain Spaulding." She was smiling though. Dave loved what she was wearing—a black flapper dress with long loops of silvery grey pearls around her neck. She looked like Al Capone's girl-friend. No ill-fitting baby-blue bridesmaid frocks for Helen.

They smoked two joints on the way to the prom, and each drank an airplane bottle of booze that Helen had stashed in her beaded handbag. Dave had Canadian Club, Helen had gin, Todd got stuck with the Grand Marnier. It was a humid eve-ning, and the air smelled like new flowers that had just yawned open. The three were pleasantly buzzed by the time they arrived at school. Helen stood on the sidewalk and smoked a cigarette in a long cigarette holder, then they all sprayed

Binaca and chewed Bubblicious and proceeded inside. A security guard checked them to make sure they weren't smuggling in booze or drugs.

"Silly guard," whispered Todd as they moved down the hall toward the auditorium. "He has totally underestimated my desire for prom drunkenness."

"Oh really?" said Helen, brightening. She eyed Todd's voluminous suit. "What do you have, a wineskin taped to your thigh?"

"No, I'm just happy to see you," said Todd, and they all laughed way too hard because they were stoned and giddy, and dressed in costume, and high school was almost a memory, and the auditorium had been transformed into a twinkly magical place lit by thousands of pale blue mini-lights, and because Todd had taken measures to keep them feeling buoyant by stashing a bottle of vodka in the wings of the stage, under a pile of props—specifically, secreted inside a somewhat soiled parasol from the year-end production of *Hello, Dolly!*

All was well. All was well.

And there was dancing. Much dancing in the centre of the hectic hot crowd. And Helen looked amazing and moved beautifully, and Dave could smell her perfume, which smelled nice—like freshly sliced lemons—and he was pretty sure she danced more toward him than Todd when they were all dancing together, and then drifted effortlessly into his arms, somehow arrived there naturally, and slow-danced with him when "These Are the Moments" came on (and was she pushing against his hard-on accidentally or on purpose a couple of times?). And she slipped off to the bathroom the next time a slow song started, so that Todd didn't get a turn. And Dave was feeling optimistic and horny as he swallowed warm vodka from his plastic cup, and undulated in the underwater blueness of the dimly lit room, until the music stopped abruptly and Ms. Keith, in a searing blast of feedback and white spotlight, leaned into the DJ's microphone and announced that Dave Burke needed to proceed to the front entrance of the school immediately.

Adrenalin. Confusion. The white light illuminating his friend's faces—Todd's scared; Helen's concerned—before it popped off and the room resumed its blue murk and music.

Dave walked hesitantly at first, trying to figure things out—realizing in a matter of moments that he wasn't, in fact, being summoned to the door because he had been drinking and was stupidly intoxicated, but that something much more dire was occurring. And he stumbled stunned and disoriented down the bright hallway, past the flesh-coloured, strangely vivid lockers, wondering who had died, and seeing flashes of his house in flames, and his parents bleeding and tangled in a horrifying car wreck.

But there were no sombre police officer waiting at the entrance. Just Mr. Hanomansing, the sometimes phys. ed, sometimes science teacher, reading a Robert Ludlum novel, and the security guard who had frisked him on the way in.

"I'm Dave Burke," said Dave, wondering just how drunk he looked and sounded.

The guard said, "Your uncle is outside. He says he has urgent news for you."

"My uncle?" said Dave. He didn't have an uncle. He had three aunts. One single, one divorced, one widowed.

Mr. Hanomansing, sensing something was amiss, set down his Ludlum and said, "If you leave the premises, you won't be readmitted."

"Well...can I just look outside and make sure it's not an emergency?"

"Your uncle can come to the door and tell you his news. If you leave the school, you can't come back in." Mr. Hanomansing stood and hitched up his Dockers. He followed Dave through the foyer to the propped-open doors of the main entrance.

Dave looked outside. There was nobody waiting there. Neither was there anyone on the paved walkway that led to the school. But past the parking lot, on the other side of the street, there was a man bent over, rummaging around in his car. Dave saw ass and legs, basically, in too-tight acid-wash jeans, and giant white sneakers that seemed to be radiating in the street-lamp light. The car was white with black stripes. Vintage. A muscle car.

In the precise moment that a vodka-sopped synapsis succeeded in firing in Dave's brain and was about to make a connection between the car across the street and Murray Mortenson's frequently mentioned Camaro z-28, the man found what he was looking for—a large pizza box—and pulled it out of the car.

"Hey, Dave-o!" he shouted when he caught sight of Dave at the entrance. "Is that you, man?!"

"Yeah," said Dave, feeling alarmed and disoriented, especially with Mr. Hanomansing looming behind him.

"Speeee-yeshull delivery!" cried Murray Mortenson in a funny Billy "AWOL" Jones voice. He hoisted the pizza box high in the air just like Billy used to do.

Dave steadied himself on the door frame.

"If you leave the premises," said Mr. Hanomansing, folding his arms across his chest, "you will *not* be allowed back in."

BECAUSE HE WAS fucked up on vodka and the lingering effects of pot oil mixed with tobacco, Dave wasn't sure exactly how weird it was to be driving around in Murray Mortenson's z-28, with an autographed pizza box on his lap, instead of attending his prom. He had not wanted to leave the prom. Not by a long shot. No. But he pretty much had to, given the circumstances. Or did he? He was too high to know.

"So listen, dude, don't take this the wrong way, OK, but with a tux like that I'm not surprised you didn't get a date for the prom." Mortenson laughed. "No offence, man."

But I did have a date, thought Dave. I had Helen. Drunk, supple, pressing-against-my-boner-a-couple-times Helen.

"Your dad make you wear that?"

"No. I rented it." Maybe she was pressing up against Todd right now. There was a lot of vodka left in that parasol.

"Oh man, you paid good money for that?" Mortenson guffawed. "I'm afraid to see your street clothes. I might have to take you to the mall tomorrow. Get you set up."

Dave thought, *You're* going to take *me* to the mall? Look at your pants. Look at your legs straining against them like sausages about to burst their acid-wash casings. And who tucks a T-shirt into their jeans? Or wears a belt covered in chunks of turquoise? He said, "My regular clothes are pretty normal."

"Glad to hear it, man. So, where is this place again?"

"Just up ahead. Past these lights, at the next major intersection.

Mortenson sped along Dupont Street. He got a spot directly outside the Vesta Lunch. "Reputable since 1955," he said, reading the sign on the way in. "What they don't tell ya is they've been open since 1940, and the first fifteen years were just fuckin' slop." Mortenson laughed loud at his own joke.

Several customers looked up when they entered. An old man in a porkpie hat eyed Dave's tuxedo with mild interest. A middle-aged woman smiled a small smile. The proprietor behind the counter didn't appear to notice. Dave figured his tux wouldn't register as strange compared to some of the things he had seen in the twenty-four-hour diner.

The smell of frying food kick-started Dave's munchies. He ordered a banquet burger, fries, and a large 7-Up. Mortenson had a cheeseburger, onion rings, and a vanilla milkshake.

"Mmm. Mighty fine," said Mortenson, jawing his burger. "But I hate these fuckers." He pulled the plastic straw out of his drink and laid it beside his plate. "Never use the things."

Dave tried not to look at the milkshake sliding off the straw and pooling on the counter. Creamy things sometimes made him feel nauseous, and he'd had a lot to drink. He focused on his fries.

"So," said Mortenson. "I guess you were surprised to see me, huh?"

"Fuck yeah. Totally."

Mortenson laughed. He took a big sip of milkshake. "I figured it'd be cool for Billy 'AWOL' Jones to deliver your graduation gift in person."

"It was. Very cool," said Dave, looking away, concentrating on his plate. Mortenson's upper lip was covered in a creamy milkshake moustache. There was a bit of mustard mixed in there too. And his face was shiny with sweat. Dave tried to think of unnauseating things, like clear mountain streams, icebergs, clean white snow. "How did you find me there anyway?"

"When we talked the other night, you told me your prom was Saturday. I knew your address, so I just MapQuested to your house and then drove around the 'hood until I found the high school. A couple people on the street helped me out."

"Hmm."

"Of course, I had no idea if the prom was going to be held at your school. Sometimes they do them at banquet halls and such, in which case I would have been shit out of luck. But I figured, what the hell, I'm coming to Toronto anyway. Might as well try to find you. And hey, I lucked out."

"Cool," said Dave.

"You know that Deluca's World Famous #1 Pizza box is one of only ten left on the planet."

"Really?"

"I know, because I have eight at home, and my ex has one."

"Wow. I appreciate it, man."

"Well, I knew you would." Mortenson chomped thoughtfully through an onion ring. "Wish I had scooped more when I had the chance. There were about forty or so left when the show ended, but I only scooped ten."

"That's a drag."

"Yeah. I wasn't really thinking about the future. I guess the rest were just destroyed."

"Hmm. So, why did you have to come to Toronto?"

"Well actually," said Mortenson raising his voice, "I have a meeting with an agent on Monday morning."

"Oh. Cool."

"Yeah. After our talk the other night, I decided to get pro-active about my career. I mean, why spin my wheels in Rochester when Toronto is so close? You know what they call your city, don't you?"

"Um—"

"'Hollywood *North*.'"

"Yeah, I've heard that."

"So I got on the horn, talked to some agents, told them I used to be a star on a very successful American sitcom," said Mortenson in his too-loud voice. Again, the old man in the porkpie hat looked over with mild interest, the middle-aged woman smiled a small smile; the proprietor behind the counter didn't appear to notice. "One of them, a very nice gal by the name of Stacey Shapiro, remembered the show fondly and invited me in for a chat. So I'll take a meeting and see what happens."

"That's great."

"Yeah."

"But wouldn't it make more sense for you to go to New York for work?"

"Hell, no. Toronto's way closer. Plus I got a good buddy here to hang out with when the jobs start rolling in."

"Oh really?"

Mortenson laughed. "Don't look so surprised. I'm talking about *you*, man."

"Oh...sorry."

"You're pretty snockered, huh?"

"I guess."

"Good times," said Mortenson with a knowing smile and a nod of the head.

Dave thought about the prospect of having to spend time with this man on a regular basis. Then he tried to imagine Mortenson getting work of any kind in television or film. The once cute teen had morphed into a truly ugly adult. He still sported the same 1980s haircut—short on the sides and poofy on top—but his hairline had receded badly and the chestnut locks had been dyed an unnatural, unvarying shade of chocolate brown. Mortenson's formerly angular face was now puffy and unhealthy-looking, the eyes bloodshot and red-rimmed. His body was pumped up—big biceps bulging out of too-short T-shirt sleeves—but at the same time over-weight, bloated-looking His clothes and pinky ring were too tight, and every part of him appeared swollen and straining, like if you pricked him with a fork, liquid would gush out and he'd deflate to the size of a regular human. No wonder he'd been doing nothing but voice-overs, thought Dave.

"You know the far-out part about the Toronto agent thing," said Mortenson, licking ketchup off an onion ring, "is that I'm dual. Did I ever mention that my mom was born in Canada?"

"Um...yeah, I think so."

"We never came up here much. Just to go shopping at that Eaton's mall once every few years. My mom's people were from Manitoba. Have you ever been there?"

"No."

"Me neither. I think I might have some great-aunt or something still there." Mortenson sniffed a bit, then wiped his face with a ketchup-stained serviette. Dave thought maybe he had cleaned off the milkshake/mustard moustache, so he risked a look. Bad idea. Mortenson had only succeeded in smearing everything together—mustard, ketchup, milkshake, snot. Dave felt his stomach roil. He lurched out of the diner and, in full sight of its occupants through the giant picture window, sprayed vomit onto the sidewalk. Cheeseburger, fries, and large 7-Up shot out of his gut like a bullet from a gun. The puke hit the pavement in one hot blast, splattering back onto Dave's face, hair, and tuxedo.

Mortenson laughed and gave Dave a thumbs-up. And for the third time in less than an hour, the man in the porkpie hat looked over with mild interest; the middle-aged woman smiled a small smile; the proprietor behind the counter didn't appear to take notice.

CONSIDERING THE VAST volume of vodka consumed, Dave felt not too horrid when he awoke at twenty minutes past noon on Sunday morning. He was ferociously thirsty and reeked of vomit and sweat, but the nausea of the previous night was gone. He ran the bathroom tap till the water was beautifully cold and then drank and drank. After a shower he felt nearly normal. No headache even, just a persistent fogginess of the

brain. Many of the prom night details were murky. Specifically, getting home and getting undressed and into bed. He
needed ibuprofen. And Coca-Cola. He needed food.

His parents were at the kitchen table, having lunch and
reading the weekend newspapers. "So," said his mother, scru-
tinizing him as he fished sandwich materials from the fridge.
"How was it?"

"It was OK," he said. "Are we out of pickles?"

"I just bought some," said his father.

Dave continued his search.

"So what was it like?" asked his mom. "Did you have fun?
Did you dance?"

"Yeah. It was pretty good."

"That's it? Just pretty good?"

"Yeah. I mean, it was all right. You know…it's not such a
big thing."

"You were home earlier than we expected."

"You were waiting up?" said Dave. "What is this, *Leave it to
Beaver*?"

"We were watching a movie," said his father.

"A very long movie." His mother laughed.

"I told you we should've just rented it. When you watch it
with commercials it's a bloody hour longer."

"Yeah, but it's free. Plus, when are we going to rent it?
When was the last time we went to the video store to rent a
video?"

"DVD," said Dave. "Videos are done."

"Yes, well," said his mom. "I still call CDs 'albums.'" She
laughed.

"Did you know that prom is short for promenade?" said his father. "And that they started up in the 1920s as a way to teach social skills to teens?"

"Dad, you told me that, like, two days ago."

"I know. I just wanted to see if you were paying attention."

Dave picked up his plate and his pop. "I'm going to eat at my computer."

"All right," said his father. "So you had a good time?"

"It was OK," said Dave.

The first thing he did was check his e-mail. There was one from Todd, wondering what the fuck had happened to him at the prom and if everything was cool. Dave phoned his friend— it was easier to tell than type—but there was no answer on his cell or home line. Probably still sleeping, thought Dave, judging by the hour he'd sent the inquiry—3:47 a.m. Dave wolfed down his food. He had an English exam the following morning that he needed to study for. It would also be his last chance to hand in his analysis of Shakespeare's Sonnet 29 to Mrs. Applebaum. He hadn't started that yet. But he only needed two double-spaced pages. He could do it later in the afternoon. And study after dinner. The prom ended at 1:00. Todd's e-mail was sent at 3:47. Had anything happened with Helen in the interim?

"Where are you going?" said his mother, who was also heading out the front door.

"Todd's," said Dave. He sat down on the porch steps and tied up his running shoes.

"Don't you have exams this week?"

"I'm just going for a half an hour."

"All right." His mother sighed. "Make sure you're home for dinner. Auntie Sam is coming and we're barbecuing."

"Ribs?"

"Yup. Seven-ish."

"I'll be there!"

His mother smiled. "Do you want a ride?"

"Nah. I need some air."

"All right. I'll see you later."

"See you."

Dave started walking down Roseman Avenue toward Yonge Street. A few seconds later he noticed a distinctive white-and-black striped z-28 parked on the street about ten cars up ahead. He froze for a moment, then wheeled around just in time to see his mom's Mazda pass him with a jaunty little honk. He threw his arm up in a hailing motion, but his mom must have thought it was a wave and kept driving. *Shit.* He ran forward a few steps, signaling frantically, but she obviously wasn't looking in the rear-view mirror. Dave glanced at the z-28. He could see now that Mortenson was in the driver's seat. Had he witnessed the escape attempt? Was he looking at Dave looking at him? Dave couldn't tell. But it was likely too late to turn on his heel and bolt in the opposite direction. Dave kept walking. As he got closer to the car, he noticed that Mortenson wasn't moving. Now he could see that his head was slumped forward and to the left, dangling in a very uncomfortable-looking manner. Was he asleep? Dead? Either way, Dave felt an instant lifting of the spirits. He would deal with Mortenson later. He trod softly as he made the car's front bumper, but just as he was about to breeze past, some kind of freaky radar kicked in and Mortenson's head bobbed upright. His eyes locked upon Dave.

"Dave-o, man...Hey!"

"Hey." Dave leaned down and peered in through the open window. The interior of the car smelled like body odour and hops. Mortenson looked disoriented. He swabbed white foam out of the corners of his mouth.

"Jesus fuck, it's hot." Mortenson got out of the car and stretched. Dark Rorschachs of sweat under bulging muscle arms. Dave noticed he was wearing the same clothes he had on last night. "What the fuck time is it, man?"

Dave pulled out his cellphone to check. "I think it's around one-thirty."

"No way."

"Yeah. It's one-thirty-nine."

"Holy shit. No wonder I need coffee. Gotta take a wicked piss too." Mortenson winced and executed a kind of mini-plié. "Is that your place right up there?"

"Um, yeah. But I was just heading out."

"Oh. Where are you going?"

"My friend Todd's."

"Mind if I tag along? I can grab a java on the way. You're heading to the corner, right? Where all them stores are?"

"Um, yeah."

"All right, let's motor. I gotta piss something fierce."

As they walked toward Yonge Street, Dave thought about all the ironic celebrity booty on display in Todd's Lair. Even an individual as oblivious as Mortenson would put two and two together if he eyeballed that stuff. He would have to keep him out of there. He would call Todd while Mortenson was finding someplace to pee and warn him about the impending visit.

"So how do you feel, man? Did you sleep it off?"

"Yeah. I feel not too bad."

"I found an excellent pub after I dropped you at home. Just up the street there."

"Oh yeah?"

"You ever go to the Rose and Crown?"

"Um, no."

"Really? You should check it out, man. It's, like, a ten-minute walk from your house. What are you waiting for?"

Dave shrugged. "I think I went there once—it was a while ago—and I got carded. We usually go to a place called the Queen's Legs."

"Well, I don't know about that place, but the Rose and Crown is great. I mean, the beer is kind of pricey compared to home—and they measure the shots right to the ounce—but the people are nice. Great bunch of folks. I closed the place down last night."

"Oh yeah? So you slept in your car?"

"Yeah. I mean, what the fuck. I was too zonked to start looking for a motel at three in the morning. It was tough enough finding my wheels." Mortenson laughed. "Thought I was going to have to crash in the park for a while there. Oh well. I saved myself fifty bucks."

"I think hotels in Toronto cost more than that. You probably saved yourself a hundred and fifty."

"Are you shittin' me, man? Jeez Louise." Mortenson chewed a hangnail. His brow creased, and he went silent for a while.

When they made the corner, Dave directed him to a Tim Horton's across the street. Then he called Todd. He got the machine.

"Wake the fuck up, man! I'm on my way over there with Murray Mortenson. I'm not shitting you, OK? He showed up at the prom last night. It was fuckin' surreal. Anyway, we're going to be at your place in ten minutes. So don't answer the door. Or just come outside, 'cause I don't want him to see all the shit in The Lair. He thinks I'm this big fuckin' fan who has never written to anyone else. You know what I mean, OK? I hope you get this."

As Dave was pocketing his cellphone, something small and dark whizzed by his head. He looked up and saw Murray Mortenson trying to jaywalk across Yonge Street. He was trapped in the middle of four lanes of traffic. He was grinning. He had a coffee and a bag of Timbits in one hand. He popped a vanilla Timbit into his mouth and then fired another chocolate one at Dave. Dave shielded his face, but the confection hit him squarely in the chest, leaving a sugar mark just above the solar plexus.

"Bull's eye!" shouted Mortenson, darting across the street with a laugh.

He'll be gone tomorrow, thought Dave, as he mustered a good-sport smile for his new friend.

TODD, APPARENTLY, GOT the message. He was waiting for them outside. He was waiting with a video camera poised. He started taping as they made their approach.

"What the hell?" said Mortenson, pushing out his chin and pulling in his gut.

"Sorry. I told him you were coming. I guess he's all excited."

"Here they are!" shouted Todd, coming down the porch steps with the camera floating a few inches in front of his face. He moved across the lawn and met them at the sidewalk. "Mr. Murray Mortenson, a.k.a. *Billy 'AWOL' Jones*, and Mr. Dave Burke."

"How ya doing?" said Mortenson in his announcer voice. "Nice to meet you."

"Murray, Todd. Todd, Murray," said Dave, trying not to smirk. Todd's faux-earnest "fan" face made him want to burst out laughing.

"Great to meet you, man," said Todd. "How cool is this?!"

Mortenson smiled. He smoothed back the sides of his hair.

"Hey, Billy," said Todd in a goofy sitcom voice. "What took you so long with that pizza?"

"Um…" said Mortenson, playing along. He did AWOL's signature shoulder shrug. "I was actually here a half hour ago, Mr. B, I just forgot to bring the pizza, so I had to go back."

Todd laughed. "Great stuff, man! That's awesome."

"Good times," said Mortenson. He smiled. He nodded. A moment later, he coughed.

"OK," Dave said. "Maybe you should…" He slid his finger across his throat in a gesture for his friend to stop filming.

"Oh come on. It's not every day a big celebrity comes waltzing down my street. Cut me some slack, Jack."

"It's all right," said Mortenson. "Part and parcel, man. I just wish I grabbed a shower this morning. Probably look like dreck warmed over."

"No, guy. You look fab," said Todd. "You haven't aged a bit."

Dave watched Todd work the zoom button, moving in to get the wrinkles and thinning hair up close.

"So what have you superstars been doing? What have I missed?"

"Not much, man. Just coffee and doughnuts this morning." Mortenson laughed. "But I guess you missed your buddy chundering on the sidewalk last night."

"No way," said Todd. "Too funny!" He zoomed out wide to get Dave in the shot.

"How about you?" said Dave. "How was the rest of the prom?"

"It was good, except we were, like: what the fuck happened to Dave?"

"So...did you guys stay late?"

"To the bitter end."

"Oh yeah? And then what?"

"Then I escorted Miss Helen to her homestead."

Dave nodded, waiting in vain for more information. "So...was Helen trashed?"

"Totally, man. Hilariously trashed. It was a beautiful thing."

"What do you mean?"

"What do you mean 'What do I mean'?"

"Well, you know...I don't know...Did something unusual happen?"

"You mean like did I throw her down in the park on the way home and get my dinky stinky? Sorry guys, I don't kiss and tell." Todd laughed but then stopped abruptly. "Ooh!" he said. "Check out the scowl. I think someone's in looove."

"Fuck off," said Dave. He glared at his friend, who was working the zoom button again, moving closer and closer until Dave's reddening face filled the frame.

THEY ENDED UP AT THE CN Tower. Even though Dave had kept trying to get away to go study, and Mortenson made repeated attempts to steer the trio toward the Rose and Crown, Todd was determined to film his "Billy 'AWOL' Jones in Toronto" video, and had succeeded—with a lot of cajole—in persuading the other two to go along with it. First they got shots of Mortenson greeting people in front of Casa Loma, then they got him ribbing a mime artist in Dundas Square, and finally they shot him smiling and waving atop the world's tallest free-standing structure. Todd wanted to continue with a stop at City Hall, but Mortenson's thirst prevailed and the z-28 headed north to Yonge and Eglinton and his pub of choice.

When the pitcher of Moosehead arrived, Dave eyed it queasily. "You know, I think I changed my mind." He pushed his glass to the other side of the table.

"Oh come on," said Mortenson, snatching it up and filling it with draught. "You gotta get back up on that horse, man." He hoisted the glass toward the camera lens. "*Cheers*," he said before setting it down in front of Dave.

"Well, maybe just a couple sips…I have an English exam tomorrow morning"

"How about you?" said Mortenson, expertly tilting and pouring another glass.

"Sure thing," said Todd. "And what about food? You guys wanna order some nachos or something?"

"I actually have to be home for dinner pretty soon. My Aunt Sam's coming for a barbecue."

"Ribs?" said Todd.

"Yeah."

"No way! Oh man! The first rib barbie of the season." Todd turned off the camera and set it on the table. "Dave's mom makes the best ribs on the planet. You have to invite us, dude. I'm salivating already."

"Um...I don't know."

"Oh come on," said Todd. He kicked Dave's foot under the table. "We can keep filming that way." Earlier in the day, Todd had pulled Dave aside to let him know that they were getting "video gold." Todd was certain that their Mortenson footage, once edited for extra hilarity, was going to garner millions of hits on YouTube, if not net them actual dollars from *Entertainment Tonight* or a gossip site like TMZ.

"It can't hurt to ask, right? Your mom's usually cool about that stuff."

Another nudge under the table. "I guess," said Dave.

"Nothing better than ribs," said Mortenson, patting his belly. "Ribs are my favourite. I fuckin' *love* ribs!"

DAVE THOUGHT IT was going to be difficult to explain—the forty-something stranger with the beer breath and the Danzig T-shirt, but Auntie Sam was a television junkie who almost instantly recognized Billy "AWOL" Jones, which went a long way toward breaking the ice with his parents. Still, first his father (in a private moment in the kitchen) and then his mother (hushed tones by the barbecue) wanted to know exactly how and why Dave had come to be hanging around with a man who was a lot closer to their age than his. The way Dave explained it, he and Todd were genuine fans of the show—fervent ones—and Mortenson had very kindly agreed to meet up to deliver autographed souvenirs while he was in town on business.

They seemed to buy it. And aside from an awkward moment off the top when Mortenson asked how Grandma was doing—Dave kicked him and whispered that nobody wanted to talk about it right now—Mortenson helped immeasurably by putting everyone at ease. He really worked the crowd. He ate more ribs than anyone, swore up and down that they were the best he had ever tasted, pressed Dave's mom for the recipe, and enthusiastically wrote it out by hand. He flirted good-naturedly with Auntie Sam and answered all her salacious questions about the various cast members of *Mother Knows Better*. He commiserated with Dave's sister, Kate, about her long-distance relationship, and then loaned her his cellphone so she could sneak off and call her boyfriend in Vancouver for free. He even bonded with Dave's father, an historian who specialized in battles and wars of the nineteenth century. As a young man, Mortenson had spent one spring and summer travelling across the United States, playing a Confederate soldier in various cavalry battles of the Gettysburg Campaign. They discussed at length the minutiae of several of those skirmishes. Finally, Mortenson won over just about everyone by cleaning up almost all of the dinner dishes, scraping and rinsing them before piling them skilfully in the dishwasher. The barbecue went on much longer than usual, and by the time it was over, everyone was feeling fairly comfortable with Murray Mortenson. That's when he chose to bring up the fact that he had an important meeting with an agent in the morning, but no hotel room yet, and could anyone recommend something modest but clean that he might attempt to book at this relatively late hour.

Aunt Sam piped up immediately. She'd had two glasses of white wine—a glass and a half more than her limit. "If you don't mind sleeping on a pullout couch, you're welcome to sleep at my condo."

Dave's mom looked shocked, as if her sister had just invited Mortenson to lick whipped cream off her body.

"You'd have your own bathroom," said Aunt Sam.

"Wow. Great. That'd be great," said Mortenson. "Thanks."

"We have a futon in the basement, Murray," said Dave's mom, who had been exchanging concerned looks with her spouse. "You could stay here if you want to."

Now it was Aunt Sam's turn to look surprised.

"It would be more comfortable than a pullout couch, and you're already here."

"True," said Mortenson. "And to be honest, I am pretty bagged. It might be a good idea to hit the sack right away so I can be fresh for my meeting in the morning. Beauty sleep, as it were." He laughed. "You don't mind, do you, Sam?"

"Of course not," she said with a rigid smile.

"Then it's settled," said Dave's mom.

DAVE GOT FRESH bedding for the futon and carried it down to the basement. He found Mortenson aiming a rifle at his chest, a Grenadiers bearskin hat sitting tall atop his head.

"You'd better put that shit away before my dad sees you. He'll have a heart attack."

"Oh. Sorry, man." Mortenson set the musket back on its custom-made mount. "This is like the one I used in re-enactments, except mine had a bayonet on it. Have you ever fired it?"

"No. It's a replica. I mean, the mechanisms work, but it doesn't take ammo."

"What's the deal with the hat?" Mortenson checked himself out in the full-length mirror on the back of the rec room door.

"It's a replica. Bearskin. British. It's worth about a thousand bucks. We're not supposed to touch it."

"Oh shit." Mortenson had to duck down to remove the improbably long hat. "Heavy sucker," he said, placing it carefully on its table in the corner. "Your dad's quite the collector, huh?"

"He was for a while. He doesn't really do it any more."

"Jeez Louise, look at all this stuff." Mortenson examined the assortment of military antiques on display. "Some of it looks real." He picked up a pair of epaulets.

"Those are real. So are those."

"What, the snowshoes?"

"Yeah. They were used by some battalion in the war of 1812."

"Cool."

"I guess. If you're into that."

"These look real old too."

"Yeah. They're Royal Navy sea service pistols."

"Beauty! He still has the whole kit. Even the lead shot."

Dave shrugged.

"Those must be worth a lot."

"I don't know. My mom's always on him to sell this shit so we can go on vacation."

"Is this a Canadian uniform?"

"British Regular. But Canadians wore them. That one's a replica."

"Hmm."

"OK. There you go." Dave placed a clean towel on the freshly made futon bed. "Bathroom's in there if you want a shower."

"Thanks, man. This is great. You got a real nice family."

"Thanks."

"And your sister's a hottie."

"I'll take your word for it."

"And your buddy Todd is a blast."

"Yeah."

Mortenson sat down on the edge of the futon. "Comfy."

"All right, I should head up. I was supposed to write an essay tonight. And study. I'll see you in the morning, OK?"

"Yeah." Mortenson stretched out on the futon. "You know, I'm having a real good time here in T.O. Maybe if that agent can get me work, I could stay for a while. You've got the summer off. We could have a lot of laughs."

Dave felt a constriction in his stomach. "Well, we'll see how it goes, I guess. OK, goodnight."

"Hey, wait a sec." Mortenson sat up. "I've got to get my stuff from the car. Can you give me a hand?"

Dave had a vision of bringing his father's Scottish Highland officer's broadsword swiftly down onto Mortenson's head. He said, "Yeah, OK. Let's go."

"I'm parked pretty close to the corner. We could grab a quick one at the Rose and Crown while we're out there."

"No, man. I just told you I have to study!"

"OK. Chill. It was just a suggestion." Mortenson stood in front of the mirror and fluffed the top of his hair. "You don't have to get pissy." He retucked his shirt into his jeans.

Dave sighed. "Let's just go, OK?"

It was close to 11:00 p.m. by the time Dave got back to his room. There wasn't enough time to write his essay, catch up on his studying, and still get a decent night's sleep. He didn't function well without proper sleep. He decided to cram for the exam, and pretend he had forgotten the essay at home. He would dream up an excuse in the morning. Mrs. Applebaum liked him. She wanted him to succeed. He would offer to bring in the essay the following day. He knew that Todd's English exam was on Tuesday afternoon. He could drop it off then. He fished his English textbook out of his backpack and got into bed with it. He tried not to think about Murray Mortenson two floors down, breathing in his basement. Dave kept glancing at the closed door. At the doorknob. He expected movement at any moment. Mortenson bursting in for some harass or harangue. But it didn't happen. For the first time in a long time, Dave was left blissfully alone. He read what he needed to read and was asleep by 1:00 a.m.

IT WAS A PECULIAR sight: Mortenson in a greenish-grey suit, eating Cheerios and drinking coffee with Dave's family. The suit had a bizarre sheen to it, the fabric reflecting purple and gold when the light hit it just so—like a bluebottle fly. And while the thing may have fit Mortenson in some previous decade, his flesh was now straining against it—seams pulling, threads tested. And he was wearing too much cologne. Dave could smell it long before he stepped into the kitchen. A wall of reek. A cloud of desperate. It put him off his breakfast. He grabbed a can of Coke and some granola bars to eat on his way to school. He wished Mortenson luck with his meeting, and said he would call to see how it went when he was finished his exam—around 10:00 a.m.

He was hoping that would be their final point of contact. He was hoping the agent would have nothing for him. Dave had had just about all the Murray Mortenson he could stand. And he had all the tape recordings and video footage and silly souvenirs he could ever possibly need from Billy "AWOL" Jones. He wanted him out of Toronto as soon as possible. He wanted him out of his life.

Dave felt a blast of adrenalin as he entered the classroom and caught sight of Helen in a tight black tank top. She gave him a concerned, inquiring smile, but he didn't respond. It took several seconds for his vision and thoughts to focus and return to normal. Helen had never worn a tank top to school before. She didn't even wear T-shirts, unless she had a long-sleeved shirt on underneath. Dave glanced at her bare arms and the back of her neck. The word *slender* entered his head.

She started to turn around, and he looked quickly away. He could feel her watching him, wanting to say something, but he kept his eyes fixed on the blank back of the exam on his desk. Had Helen slept with Todd after the prom? Did the sexy shirt signal some kind of fundamental change? He didn't have time to ponder it because the second hand bumped its way to the top of the clock and it was 9:00 a.m. and Mrs. Applebaum instructed everyone to turn their tests over and begin.

For an hour there was nothing but ballpoints routing paper, and Mrs. Applebaum cracking her gum at regular intervals. Dave didn't mind the sound. He liked it. And the exam was easier than expected, though it took him the full allotment of time to complete. He handed it to his teacher with an exaggerated flourish. "Mrs. Applebaum," he said as he looped it through the air and into her hand.

"Mr. Burke," she said with a wry smile, accepting the test and placing it on the pile on her desk.

"Before I head off on my madcap summer adventures, I want to thank you for being a most inspiring educator, and wish you a fruitful and invigorating vacation."

Mrs. Applebaum smirked and cracked her gum. "Do you have anything else for me?" she said, eyeing Dave's backpack.

Dave did his best to appear bewildered. Then he winced as if pierced by the sudden memory of his assignment.

"Damnations!" he cried. "My sonnet essay. Two double-spaced pages of trenchant, highly original analysis, and I forgot it at home. What a boob!"

Mrs. Applebaum seemed amused. "Well, it's a good thing you live close by," she said. "Before you head off on your madcap summer adventures, why don't you dash home and retrieve that highly original essay. I'll wait here."

"You would do that?" said Dave, trying to buy time to formulate an excuse.

"I would," said Mrs. Applebaum, her eyes twinkling. "I can get a jump start on my marking." She tapped the pile of tests on the desk.

"All right," said Dave. He was busted and she was playing with him. Maybe if he could make it enjoyable enough she wouldn't kill him and eat him. He turned to exit, then stopped abruptly in the doorway. "Oh shoot!" he said. "Darn it! I'm afraid I'm going to have to bring that trenchant, highly original essay in tomorrow."

"Is that a fact?"

"Yes. Silly me. I just remembered I have an appointment at 10:30 a.m. sharp."

"Really?" Mrs. Applebaum smiled. "And what appointment would that be?"

"Um…" He had to think of something funny. Something to show that he knew she was onto him, preferably something self-deprecating. "I'm booked for an extra-strength high colonic. Apparently, I'm full of…well, you know."

Mrs. Applebaum cracked her gum. "I see."

"So how about it? Can I bring the essay in tomorrow afternoon?"

"No you may not," she said, rising from her chair. Mrs. Applebaum slid the exams briskly into her briefcase. She wasn't smiling any more.

DAVE WOULD HAVE felt a lot more lugubrious had he not found Helen waiting in her big black boots on the sidewalk outside the school. She was smoking a cigarette. Her cargo pants were orange. She looked very Halloween.

"Hey," she said. "How are you?"

Dave shrugged. "I'm OK."

She flicked away her cigarette. "Is everything all right? I was worried about you the other night."

"Oh…Yeah. That was weird. Um, everything's OK though."

"Oh good. I thought maybe…you know, something bad had happened. "

"Yeah, me too. It freaked me out when they called my name. I was, like, *what the fuck*? But it was just an unexpected visitor from out of town."

"Oh."

"Someone who thought it was a good idea to come and get me in the middle of the prom."

"Hmm," said Helen, nodding. Her brow furrowed.

"You know once you leave the premises they won't let you back in."

"Oh. Is that what happened?"

"Yeah. I didn't want to leave."

"Hmm. So they wouldn't let you bring her in?"

"No. It was a *him*. Not a her."

"Oh." Helen stopped herself from smiling.

"And I wouldn't bring him in even if they let me…or begged me, for that matter."

"Not your best pal then?"

"No. Hell no. It's kind of a long story. It's pretty funny actually. Do you remember a sitcom from the early eighties called *Mother Knows Better*?

"No. Lame title though."

"Yeah. Anyway, this guy used to be a child actor on that show. I wrote him a fan letter as a joke, and he was so deliriously happy about it he started writing back and calling me all the time, like four or five times a week."

"That's weird."

"Yeah." Dave laughed. "Then all of a sudden he shows up at the prom, looking for me. Well, he was in town for something else, but still..."

"So he's gay."

"No."

Helen pulled a face.

"No. He's totally straight. He was married."

"That doesn't mean anything."

"Believe me, he's straight. He just thinks I'm this huge-o fan, and that he was doing me a big favour by stopping by."

"Hmm." Helen frowned, mulling it over.

Dave's cellphone rang. "Speak of the devil." He fished it out to check the call display. "Yup," he said, turning the phone off.

"You can take it if you want."

"I'll call him later."

Helen lit another cigarette. She didn't seem to be in a hurry to get away.

"So," said Dave. "You guys stayed all the way to the end, eh?"

"Yeah, well...we were hoping you might come back."

"Oh. Todd said you got pretty trashed."

"God, yeah. I'll never drink again."

Dave laughed.

"No doubt he told you I was puking all the way home."

Dave brightened. "Really? No, he didn't tell me. So you puked repeatedly on the way home?"

"Yeah." Helen laughed. "But it didn't stop Todd from trying to kiss me when we got there."

"Oh really?" Dave laughed. He could feel himself blushing. "You're telling me he didn't tell you all this?"

"No. I think he wanted me to think the evening had ended a bit differently, if you know what I mean."

"What? Are you kidding me? What did he say?!"

"Nothing specific. It was more of a suggestive withholding of information."

"Uch. That is so fucking adolescent. And annoying!"

"Yeah well...you know what Todd's like."

"And you believed him?"

"No! I don't believe anything he says." Dave laughed.

"He's your best friend."

"Yeah. But, you know, we're different."

"Are you?" It was a serious question. Helen stared hard into his eyes—half search, half challenge. It was unsettling.

Dave said, "Yes," because she wanted him to.

Helen exhaled. Her face relaxed. "Good," she said, smiling, her usual self again. "So...what are you doing now? Are you busy?"

"Um, not really. Why?"

"My parents went to Buffalo for the day. I thought I'd grab a swim. You want to come?"

"Yeah. That'd be great."

"Great."

"Oh shoot!"

"What?"

"Um, I know this sounds weird, but I don't really want to go home right now." Murray Mortenson would probably be waiting there. Murray Mortenson would definitely be waiting there.

"So?"

"So my bathing suit's at home."

"Oh." Helen smiled. She poked him in the stomach with her index finger. "Didn't I just tell you my parents are out?"

DAVE HEARD A SPLASH. Then a few seconds later Helen's voice saying it was OK, he could turn around now. And he did. And what he saw was very fine indeed. She swam to him naked. She put her arms around his neck and her legs around his hips. They kissed. The taste of cigarettes. The smell of chlorine. Sunshine everywhere and hardly any gravity. She put her hand on his cock. "Are you a virgin?" she said. He tried hard not to come. He had come once already—in his pants by the side of the pool the first time she kissed him and pressed her hand against his crotch. Luckily, she had let him undress and slip into the water without being watched. He was able to wipe himself on his underwear and then ball up his clothes in a way in which the splooged undies could dry a bit in the sun, without her seeing anything.

"No," he said. "Are you?"

"No," said Helen. "I'm on the pill." She bit his earlobe. "So who have you had sex with?"

"Um…a few people."

"Really? Anyone I know?"

She knew he was lying; he could see that. "No. No one from school."

"Hmm. Too bad, 'cause if you were a virgin we could have sex right here without a condom."

"Really?"

"Well, unless you were worried about me. But I've only done it with one person, and we always used condoms."

"Anyone I know?"

"No. It was in Greece."

"Oh. A nice Greek boy."

"Actually, he was from Italy."

"Hmm. And do you keep in touch?"

"No. He didn't speak English."

"So you had a lot in common, eh?"

"It was a summer vacation, wiseass, we didn't need to."

"Hmm."

"But you've had sex with a few people, huh?"

"Well, maybe not 'a few.' Maybe it was more like…none."

She laughed. "Honestly?"

"Yeah. Although I could have with Mindy McMachon. She wanted to."

"Yeah well, that's hardly surprising."

"I didn't want to though."

"Was it the bad skin or fear of disease?"

"Neither. It was the smile. When she smiles she looks like my Aunt Sam. They have the same mouth."

"Ew. Weird."

"Yeah. The tiny teeth and the big gums."

"Hmm. Otherwise you would have banged her?"

"Probably."

"Well, I'm glad you didn't." She licked his neck.

"Oh yeah?"

"Yeah." She took his cock and awkwardly guided him into her. He was shocked at how warm she felt. He closed his eyes and tried not to come. He knew he was supposed to thrust, but he didn't dare move. She kissed him again. Her lips were cold now. The water was cold. But Helen was incredibly warm inside. "You feel good," she whispered. It was tricky in the pool, but he managed to execute a dozen half-decent strokes before losing his load. He apologized, but she said not to. She said he lasted longer than she expected, and that they could do it again later. She slid off him and swam toward the deep end. He went after her, grabbed her by the ankle, and pulled her back into his arms. They played in the water like that, splashing and laughing like little kids. She would swim away and he would go get her. Now that he had touched her, he couldn't stop. His hands needed to be on her. He caught her in the shallow end and floated her on her back, balancing her on his fingertips. At first she kept her arms folded across her breasts, but after a while she closed her eyes and let her arms relax to her sides as he moved her slowly through the water. It allowed him to take in the body stretched out in front of him, and it made him want to fuck again. He tried to kiss her, but she said no, not yet, that it was time to eat.

She swam underwater to the deep end, climbed the metal ladder, and wrapped herself in a beach towel—red with orange and pink flowers. "I'll be right back," she said.

Dave drifted over to the Venus de Milo statue. He sat under the mini-waterfall and let the water cascade over his head and shoulders. It felt gloriously good. He stared at the sky, blue and cloudless. It was going to be a great summer.

Helen returned with food and a bottle of mineral water. They sat on the ground in their flower towels and ate cheese and bread and spicy salami and olives and nectarines and moon-shaped almond cookies covered in powdered sugar. They swigged ice-cold Perrier straight from the bottle. When Dave had had enough to eat he reached for Helen and kissed her and tried to lower her gently onto her back. She resisted. "Let me put this stuff away first," she said.

"Do you want help?"

"No, it's OK. Back in a flash."

Dave reclined on the warm concrete and stared at his feet. They looked very white. The toenails needed a clip. He rolled onto his stomach and let the hot sun warm his back. His head rested comfortably on his arms, which smelled pleasantly of chlorine and sweat. He watched an ant drag a crumb twice its size. Dave sighed. He had never felt so relaxed, so completely content. That's when Helen came screaming through the sliding glass doors with a look of terror on her face.

"My parents are home! *Get the fuck out!*"

The privacy fence was absurdly high, impossible to scale. Dave snatched up his clothes and backpack and ran as fast he could without losing his towel toward the gate that led to the side of the house. He opened it and slipped through, praying that the parents wouldn't use the side door for some reason. He crouched close to the brick house, gripped with panic, his heart hammering. With shaking fingers he dropped his clothes on the ground and found his sticky, crusty underwear. He got them on. Then the pants and shirt. He stuffed the towel and his socks in his backpack and carried his shoes in his hand. He moved stealthily toward the front yard, pausing at the edge of the house to listen, and then peek around to make sure the coast was clear. There were a few kids Big Wheeling in a convoy down the sidewalk, and an old lady across the street, hosing down her paved front lawn. No sign of Helen's parents though. Dave made a break for it. He ran as fast as possible in bare feet, and didn't stop or turn around until he reached Roseman Avenue.

THERE WERE FIVE new messages on Dave's cellphone. The first was from Mortenson saying it was ten-fifteen, he had finished his meeting, and would head to Dave's place and see him there soon. Dave noted that he sounded uncharacteristically curt. In the next message, Mortenson was waiting on Dave's porch, wondering why it was taking him so long to return from his 9:00 to 10:00 a.m. exam. He told Dave to please call if something had come up. The message was punctuated by several sorrowful sighs. The third message was angry: "OK, *fuck this. I'm heading to the Rose and Crown.*" Click. Message number four was boozy and contrite. "*Hey, man, Murray here. Um, don't know if your phone's dead or what. Maybe some kind of emergency with your grandma again. I don't know. Anyway, I'm gonna wander over to Todd's place and see if you guys are there. OK. Um, sorry if I sound*

*fucked up, I'm just—I don't know, I'm just fuckin' bummed. All right.
Call me if you get this."* The fifth message was from Todd, saying
he was at the Rose and Crown with Mortenson who was getting "totally hammer-headed," and that he was taping it all
and it was hilarious, and to get his ass over there.

Dave found them in a booth at the back. Mortenson was
doing shots and drinking beer. He had removed his suit jacket
and tie. Todd was eating French fries with one hand and vid-
eotaping Mortenson with the other. Mortenson didn't seem
depressed. He was laughing boisterously about something
when he caught sight of Dave approaching the table.

"Hey! There he is. What the fuck took you so long?"

"Sorry about that." Dave shrugged and slid in next to Todd.

"I was just telling buddy-boy about Skanky Benson, I mean
Tracy Benson." Another exuberant guffaw. "Hey, Rita," Mortenson yelled at a passing waitress. "Another pitcher, another
glass, and another Cutty, sweetheart."

"You got it, Mur." Rita breezed off to fetch the order.

"So where were you?" said Todd, turning off the camera
and setting it on the table.

"Um, actually, I was at Helen's." Dave smiled and took a fry
from Todd's plate.

"You were at Ghost World's?"

"Yeah."

"With your phone off?"

"Yup." Dave tried to stop smiling but couldn't quite manage it. "We went for a swim."

"Fuck off! You went swimming with Helen? Who else was
there?"

"Nobody."

"Just you and Helen. And George checking on you every thirty seconds?"

"Actually, George and Uranus weren't home at the time."

"Holy fuck. Check out the shit-eating grin. I do believe our boy just got some Ghost World action."

"Oh yeah?" said Mortenson. "Did you get laid, man?"

Dave laughed. He could feel himself blushing.

"Holy shit," said Todd. "You didn't actually bag Helen, did you?!"

Dave shrugged. "I'm not saying anything."

"Oh my god. You bastard!" Todd pounded his fist on the table. "I can't believe it. After all my efforts, she picked you over me?!"

"Efforts? What efforts?"

"Hello! Supplying drugs, booze. Frequent bathing. *Efforts.*"

"Fuckin' women," said Mortenson.

"I need a drink," said Todd.

As if on cue, Rita arrived with the pitcher and the whisky. Glasses were filled and raised.

"Well, here's to at least one of us getting some pussy," said Todd with a grim grin.

"Yeah," said Mortenson. "Here's to one of us having a good fuckin' time this morning."

Dave didn't say anything—no confirmation, no denial— but he did lift his glass and clink it against the others, and he did smile smugly before taking a long cold swallow of draught.

Over the course of several pitchers, Mortenson's mood oscillated from ebullient to morose. After some urging from

Dave, he recounted his meeting with the Toronto talent agent, which started well but didn't end that way. Apparently, Stacey Shapiro was very friendly and effusive, welcoming him in, interviewing him at length about his days on *Mother Knows Better*. Unlike his Rochester agent, she didn't take calls while they were in the meeting, and she had her assistant make him a cappuccino, which was served with Italian cookies—something called biscotti. Delicious. Mortenson felt respected. He thought that Stacey Shapiro was someone he could really get with. But after close to an hour of animated chatting, when he steered the conversation away from gossip and trivia to the reason he was there—what kind of work she could find for him in town—she apologized and told him that she couldn't help him. She said she had someone very like him on her roster already, and since he would be competing for jobs with this long-term, valued client, she could not represent him. Mortenson told her he understood, and then started berating her for wasting his time. His rant concluded in a demand that she reimburse him for his round-trip Rochester–Toronto gasoline costs. When she politely declined, he fired a biscotti across her desk and told her to shove it up her ass. He kicked over a recycling bin full of empty water bottles and pop cans on his way out of the office.

Todd applauded the spontaneous outburst, but Dave thought it was misguided.

"You should have played it cool," Dave said. "This other client could've died tomorrow, or maybe he'd be busy and some other choice gig would come up and she'd think of you for it."

Mortenson laughed bitterly. "No, man. You don't get it. I've been in this business *twenty-five years*. When an agent says they have someone who's the same 'type' as you on their roster, it's bullshit. OK? It's the supposedly nice way of telling you that you suck shit and they don't want to deal with your ass."

"Are you sure about that?"

"Sure I'm sure. It's a fucking ruse. Every actor that's been around the block knows that song and dance. You think I've never heard it before?" Mortenson snorted. "I've been in this business for twenty-five years, man. But Stacey fuckin' Shapiro thinks I was born yesterday! Shit…" Mortenson's eyes closed and his head lolled forward.

"Hey, are you all right?"

The head snapped upright. "Yeah. I'm good."

"Well…screw Stacey Shapiro," said Dave, trying not to look at Todd, who was literally vibrating with suppressed laughter. "There are lots of agents in Toron—"

"No, man! It's over. So just—you know…" Mortenson sighed. "I know you're trying to help and all, but can you just not talk about it? OK?" Mortenson flagged down Rita and attempted to order another round, but he was slurring badly and his eyes were drooping shut.

"Sorry, Mur. Maybe you should take a little break. How about a cup of coffee?"

"I don't think so, lovely Rita. I think we'll just have *one* more pitcher and *one* more Cutty."

"Look—hey, can you get that camera off me, please. I don't like being filmed."

"Sorry." Todd swivelled the camera back to Mortenson.

"Listen, how about a round of coffees? My treat."

"You think I should have coffee, Rita? Maybe a nice cappuccino?"

"Sure. We can do that for you, Murray."

"And maybe some *biscotti* to go with it."

Uh oh, thought Dave. There was a lot of menace in the cookie reference.

"We don't have those. How about some cherry pie?"

"Cherry pie! Um…OK, lovely Rita. And a pitcher and a Cutty, and you can hold the pie between your knees with the fuckin' egg salad." Mortenson burped long and loud.

"All right. I think we're done here," said Rita crisply. She plucked their bill out of her waist apron, slapped it on the table, and moved off.

Mortenson leered at the video camera and gave the thumbs-up sign.

"Okey-dokey," said Dave. "Time to go."

Mortenson pulled out his wallet and squinted at the bill. "Fuckin' women," he said, throwing a handful of American twenties on the table. "My treat, boys." He scooped his suit jacket and weaved precariously toward the front entrance, oblivious to Todd and Dave, who were clutching each other, in stitches in his wake.

"Sayonara!" yelled Mortenson as he staggered out the door.

SUNSHINE. BLAZING BRIGHT and shockingly inappropriate after the dark cave of the pub. Dave felt it should have been night, but it wasn't, and as he stepped blindly onto the scorching sidewalk, he discovered he was considerably drunker than he thought, or planned on getting, and he resented it. He had a science exam and a math exam that he needed to study for, and now he would have to sober up, probably even take a nap before he could start. It would likely be after dinner before he could get anything worthwhile accomplished.

"So what do you dudes want to do?" said Mortenson, chewing a hangnail and swaying slightly on the spot.

"Nothing, man. I have to go study. I've got exams tomorrow."

"Oh come on. Don't be a pussy. Let's find another bar."

"No. You guys go ahead if you want. I need to study." Dave thought about Mrs. Applebaum's face. The pursed lips. The disappointed eyes. He put his backpack on to signal resolve.

"Actually," said Todd. "I should probably head too. I've got exams tomorrow afternoon."

"Yeah whatever," said Mortenson. He sighed. "Well, fuck it. I might as well go home too then." He dug his car keys out of his pocket and started careening down the street toward the Yonge-Roseman intersection.

"The dude can't drive," whispered Todd.

"No fucking kidding," said Dave. "You'd better come with for a bit. I might need your help."

They caught up with Mortenson and walked with him across Yonge and down Roseman to where his car was parked.

"All right, guys. It's been, as they say, a slice."

"Um, I don't think you should drive so soon," said Dave. "You've had quite a few."

"Nah, I'm good," said Mortenson, trying in vain to stab his key into the lock of the z-28.

"Here, let me help you with that," said Todd, taking the opportunity to wrest the keys from his hand and pocket them.

"Hey, what the fuck? That's not cool, man."

"No. It's *drinking and driving* that's not *cool*, 'man.'" Todd said it funny, as if he were impersonating a mental hygiene film from the 1950s.

Mortenson was not amused. "Just give me the keys, shit-smear." He lumbered toward Todd, who deked out of the way and hopped back several steps.

As hilarious as it might have been to see his skinny friend pummelled by the former sitcom star, Dave felt he should intervene.

"Hey, wait," he said. "Isn't all your stuff still in my basement?"

Mortenson paused to ponder the question. "Oh yeah. Shit..."

"We should go get it, don't you think?"

"Yeah. All right."

Todd slipped the car keys to Dave. "Well, I should probably—"

"Not yet." Dave grabbed Todd by the arm and pulled him down Roseman. As they got closer to the house, Dave spotted someone sitting on the steps of his front porch. It was Helen. Helen at his house. She had never been to his house before. He was surprised she even knew which one was his.

When she caught sight of them approaching, she stood and moved to the sidewalk. She waved. Dave waved back. His heart was jumping. A twinge of lust ricocheted through his body.

"Well, look-y who's here!" said Todd.

"Hey." Helen was smiling and blushing. "Sorry to show up unannounced."

"No, it's fine!" said Dave.

"It was kind of an abrupt send-off, so I thought I should come by for a minute." Helen laughed.

"Hey, s'that the bitch you banged this morning?"

"Excuse me?" Helen looked truly shocked.

"Uh oh," mumbled Todd, doing his best not to smirk.

Helen's expression morphed into a glare, which she fixed on Dave.

"I never said that!"

"Very mature." Helen turned and walked quickly away.

"She's better than I expected, man. *Hey, come back, gorgeous!*"

Dave took off after Helen. He had to jog to keep up with her furious strides.

"I didn't say anything, I swear!"

"Yeah right."

"I didn't! They just assumed 'cause I said I came from swimming with you."

"Yeah, everyone who goes swimming has sex."

"Look, I'm sorry! They just assumed something happened. I didn't comment one way or the other, I swear! What was I supposed to do? Deny it?"

"So you didn't imply anything, right? It all came from your little sitcom friend—who's pathetic, by the way."

"He's not my friend. He's a total fucking asshole. I can't stand him! We're only hanging out with him as a joke."

"Oh really?"

"Yes!"

"Well, that's even more pathetic." Helen stopped in her tracks and faced Dave. A constellation of hives flamed red across her left cheek. "You know, for some reason I believed it when you said you were different than Todd."

"I am."

"No. You're not. You guys present yourselves as being all alternative, but you're really just stupid little frat boys."

The words hit Dave like a punch.

"And if there's one thing this 'bitch' hates, it's fucking frat boys. Oh well. At least school's over and I don't have to see either of you again."

As Dave watched Helen run away from him, he felt as if a large hand was squeezing his heart and lungs, causing vital energy to drain from his body. He stood hopeless and helpless on the sidewalk until he saw the familiar black Blundstones disappear around the corner, taking love and summer with them. For a moment Dave thought he was going to sink onto the sidewalk and fall asleep, but then he flashed on Mortenson's drunken, bloated face and a bolt of angry adrenalin turned him around and propelled him fast down the street.

"WHAT THE FUCK IS YOUR DAMAGE, MAN?!"

"Whoa. Sorry, dude. I didn't think she could hear me." Mortenson was slumped on the front porch steps, sweating in his fly suit. Todd was seated beside him, fumbling with the video camera, trying to quickly change the battery.

"What are you talking about?! Of course she could hear you. You said it right out loud! What are you, retarded?"

"Relax, man. I'm sorry. I'm kinda trashed, OK? Just send her some flowers. It'll be fine."

"No, it won't be fine! This isn't 1950! Jesus Christ!"

"Here…" Mortenson pulled out his wallet, removed a twenty, and held it out to Dave. "Send her them roses with the long stems. Trust me."

"No, I don't trust you! I'm fuckin' sick of you!"

"Hey! Come on, Dave-o, be a pal. I'm having a shit day."

"You've been having a shit day since 1985—*which is before I was even born*. I'm not your 'pal' and I don't give a crap!" Dave vaulted up the porch steps and unlocked the front door. "You fucked up my grades, now you fucked this up. I just want you to collect your shit and get the hell out of here."

Mortenson stood and teetered on the spot. He looked bewildered. "I fucked up his grades?" he said to the camera.

Todd, filming silently, shrugged.

Mortenson gripped the porch railing and made his way up the stairs and into the house.

Todd turned off the camera. "That was harsh, dude."

"Whatever. It's time to get rid of this guy."

"You're not going to let him drive."

"I don't know. I don't fuckin' care any more. I just want him gone." Dave sank onto the porch steps and rested his head in his hands.

"Well," said Todd. "At least we got a kick-ass tape out of it. This thing's going to be bigger than the Screech sex tape. Hey, we should get him to give you a Dirty Sanchez before he goes."

"Shut the fuck up."

Todd switched the camera to standby mode. "I've got to make sure I get that final shot of him wandering away. Like the creature going back to the lagoon."

"Where the hell is he already?"

"Probably passed out down there."

"Can you go check?"

"Me? It's *your* house."

"Yeah, but I just went nuts on the guy. Come on…"

"I'm not going down there alone. The dude's a menace."

"Thanks a fuckin' lot."

"I'll look through the window, OK?" Todd stood up. "Hey, maybe I can get a shot of him packing up his stuff!" He moved around to the side of the house. A few seconds later, Dave heard, "*Holy shit!*" Then Todd came running back. "Dude, he's got one of your dad's guns and he's loading it!"

Dave stood up. "He can't be. Those things are just for show."

"Are you sure? Because he was pouring something that looked a lot like gunpowder down the barrel."

"Are you talking about the rifles?"

"No, the handguns."

Dave and Todd ran back to the window and peered through. Sure enough, Mortenson was seated at the edge of the futon with one of the Royal Navy sea service pistols wedged between his knees. The antique pistol kit was open on the bed beside him. Mortenson wrapped one of the spherical lead bullets in a piece of Kleenex and then pushed it into the mouth of the pistol. He slid a ramrod out from under the barrel and began tamping down the lead shot.

Todd pressed the video camera lens close to the window. "Are you sure that's not going to work? 'Cause it looks like he knows what he's doing."

Mortenson pulled back an iron lever, revealing a small depression in which he poured powder from a brown leather flask.

"I don't know. I mean, all that stuff's, like, two hundred years old. I can't imagine my dad would leave it there if it were dangerous."

"Well, I don't know if we should wait to find out." Todd giggled nervously. "The guy's drunk and probably pissed off at you."

Mortenson capped the flask and placed it on the bed. He stood up and cocked the hammer on the pistol.

"Shit. Maybe we should call 911?!"

Mortenson started unbuttoning his dress shirt.

"Uh oh," said Dave.

He pressed the barrel of the gun against his chest.

"Holy fuck!" said Todd.

Mortenson pulled the trigger. A flinty flash of spark and then nothing.

Todd and Dave looked at each other and laughed.

A nanosecond later: BOOM!

TWO POLICE CRUISERS, lights flashing and sirens blaring, arrived at Dave's house before the ambulance. No less than four officers leapt into action, responding to the 911 call as if Dave and Todd were warring gang members and the basement was full of snipers (instead of a prostrate former sitcom star). Todd seemed excited, almost invigorated by it all. Dave felt panicked and scared. He saw his neighbours peering at him from behind blinds and curtains, trying to determine if he was victim or perpetrator. He averted the eyes of his neighbours. He looked down at the grass, or his shoes.

It seemed to take forever for the police to establish that there was no danger of anyone else being shot in the Burke household that day. Only then were the paramedics allowed to collect Mortenson and speed him away in the ambulance. Two officers remained behind to interrogate Todd and "secure the crime scene," i.e., confiscate every one of Dave's dad's cherished antique weapons, including the decorative cannon in the corner. The other pair of officers took Dave with them to the hospital, so they could grill him further about his role in the mishap and make sure that Mortenson's gunshot wound was indeed self-inflicted.

After two hours of exhausting and humiliating questioning, during which time Dave discovered that trying to explain the Murray Mortenson story and not come off sounding like a complete jerk proved more difficult than he ever would have imagined, he was allowed to go free. The cops left without telling him anything about Mortenson's condition, so Dave had to roam the corridors and try to flag down one of the fleet-footed emergency room nurses. Eventually, a stocky redhead in lime-green Crocs slowed enough for Dave to get her attention.

"Excuse me," he said. "I'm trying to find out how a patient is doing. Murray Mortenson?"

"Are you a relative?" she asked.

"No," said Dave.

"Friend?" said the nurse, peering hard over wire-rim glasses.

Before Dave could formulate a response, an intercom voice pierced the air with a Code Blue announcement, and the lime-green Crocs flashed down the hall and disappeared between swinging doors.

Dave pictured the nurse racing to the aid of Murray Mortenson. Code Blue, obviously, was not a good thing. Dramatic resuscitation scenes played through Dave's head as he moved down the hallway and pushed through the large black doors. He came upon a nursing station with three long counters, behind which doctors and nurses conferred, or consulted clipboards, or spoke on the phone, or wrote out reports. Dave waited. He waited some more. Hospital staff breezed in and out of the station without acknowledging him. It was a full ten minutes before a nurse made eye contact, listened to his inquiries, and then summoned a Dr. Eman to provide an answer.

The doctor was short and chubby. She wore an electric-blue headscarf and was eating mini-carrots out of a baggie. She had a heavy accent. "Your friend is in surgery," said the doctor, chewing. "They must remove a lead shot that has penetrated the chest wall and lodged in the right ventricle of the heart."

"Holy—! Is he going to be all right?"

"Probably. I think so. Because he has used this round pellet instead of a regular bullet. The regular bullet moves very efficiently through bone and flesh, but not the round pellet. No."

"OK," said Dave. "So—?"

"OK," said Dr. Eman, moving swiftly down the hall.

"Um, when I can I see him?" called out Dave.

"Not for many, many hours," said the doctor before waving the baggie of mini-carrots and disappearing into a cubicle.

DAVE CALLED HOME. He thought he was going to have to explain everything that had happened, but his mother had already spoken to a police detective who had visited the house for follow-up. Dave expected large amounts of wrath. Fortunately, his mom had reserved the bulk of her fury for his dad, who had kept dangerous firearms unlocked in their rec room.

"Do you want me to pick you up?" asked his mom.

"Um, no. I think I'm gonna wait for a while."

"Fine. But not in the emergency waiting room, OK? I don't want you getting TB. Or this year's version of SARS."

Dave rolled his eyes. "I'll wait in the caf. But listen, can you do me a favour and bring my backpack down, and my math and science text books so I could study?"

His mother sighed. "I suppose. But I don't want to have to find parking at the hospital, so be outside in half an hour."

Thirty-two minutes later, Dave's mom delivered the requested items plus bottled water, a heavy sandwich wrapped in foil, two Cellophane packets of oatmeal cookies, and a purse-sized bottle of Purell. Her mouth was rigid, angry, but she hugged Dave hard and gave him money to take a taxi home if he was going to be late.

Dave tried to study for his exams. He tried and tried but couldn't concentrate. The cafeteria was loud and crowded, and the emergency department waiting room was full of sad people making sick sounds—half of them splayed out on orange vinyl couches, groaning, bleeding. Dave went outside. He doused his hands with Purell and, after a decent interval, unwrapped his sandwich. Corned beef spilled from gaping bread slices like flesh from a wound. He wrapped it back up, squeezed it tight into a foil-wrapped ball, and fired it into the garbage. He wasn't hungry anyway.

He was distinctly unhungry.

Dave slumped against the brick wall of the hospital and took out his textbooks. He tried again to read the required material, but his brain wouldn't stay with the page. It kept conjuring Helen's pale face, livid with hives. He reread the same paragraphs over and over again. The same paragraphs. Over and over.

Every couple of hours, Dave would track down the red-headed nurse to ask about Mortenson's status, and whether he could see him yet. Just before 8:00 a.m., she popped her head outside to report that Mortenson was resting comfortably in the ICU and that Dave could go sit with his friend.

"Come on," said the nurse with the lime-green Crocs. "I'll show you the way."

BLINKING LIGHTS AND little beeps and many pieces of hulking medical equipment, most of it on wheels. In the centre of it all, an old man asleep with his mouth hanging open. A pale old man who only a day earlier was Murray Mortenson, strutting. Now there were tubes running out of his nostrils, an IV protruding from his neck, and one in the back of his hand. Drip drip went the mystery liquids, through the tubes and into the man-made holes. Beep beep went the medical machines, in counterpoint to the rhythmic surf of heavy respiration.

Dave manoeuvred himself onto a lone plastic chair in the corner beside the bed.

He tried to move the chair farther back but hit wall. He felt acutely uncomfortable. There was a bag of urine hooked on the side of the bed about eight inches away from his knee. And high on Mortenson's upper right arm, Dave could see what was never meant to be seen by him—a faded, home-made tattoo in navy blue: *Tracy*.

"You know I went out with her."

Dave quaked at the sound. He hadn't noticed Mortenson waking up. "Hey, man. How are you doing?"

Mortenson's eyes closed, and his head lolled a bit to one side. "We went out for just under two weeks."

"Yeah."

"I had sex with her in an electrical field," he said woozily, his voice dropping to a whisper.

"Yeah, I know. You told me about that."

"I was seventeen. It was my first time."

Dave braced himself for the rest of the story—the inevitable tirade about skanky Tracy Benson's substandard sexual performance and body parts.

"She was only thirteen," said Mortenson, his eyes still closed. "Her teeth . . . she had these white, white teeth." Mortenson smiled. "I made her laugh, 'cause I told her the transmission towers reminded me of Jolly Green Giants. You know how that fucker stands with his hands on his hips?"

"Yeah."

"I said, Those things look like Jolly Green Giants, and she laughed and laughed…"

"Hmm."

"We were pretty stoned."

"Yeah."

"Pot and Southern Comfort. You don't get seeds in pot any more, but you used to get seeds. You'd get these seeds and they would crack when they got hot…these little crackling, popping sounds…It was weird 'cause it was like the whole electrical field was kind of crackling. It was, like, really dry and sunny and really hot, and the transmission towers were buzzing and the grasshoppers were buzzing and the bees and the wildflowers were buzzing. It was all kind of super-bright and vibrating, you know?"

Dave didn't respond. He was thinking suddenly about Helen in the swimming pool. How he balanced her on his fingertips and moved her through water. How everything shined.

"And she was so beautiful. God. You have no idea how perfect…" Mortenson smiled. A few moments later the mouth went slack and he was asleep again, as still and as pale as a corpse.

Dave stared absently at the faded tattoo. He was thinking about his moment in the pool when everything to come seemed so blue-sky happy. Dave unzipped his backpack and pulled out the crumpled beach towel—red with orange and pink flowers—that he had inadvertently stolen from Helen's. It was still damp. He brought it to his face and inhaled. It smelled like chlorine and coconut oil. It smelled like summer. He folded it up. As he was burying it deep in the black backpack, he spotted the handout from English class. The one with Shakespeare's Sonnet 29. He took it out and read it, and for the first time since he was a kid he felt tears flooding his eyes.

What was it about the poem that he had found funny before?

It didn't seem at all funny any more.

Suddenly, Dave remembered something from earlier in the day when he had raced to the basement to go to Mortenson's aid. The room smelled like sulphur and smoke. There was blood trickling onto the floor. "Did you call 911?!" he shouted to Todd. But Todd wasn't right behind him as expected. Todd was still at the window with the video camera, still filming the hilarious Billy-"AWOL"-Jones-in-Toronto movie.

Beep beep beep went the medical machines as Dave stood and put on his backpack. It was almost time to go write—and possibly fail—his exam. *See you*, he said. But there was no response. Just the pulse of machine.

As Dave left the hospital, he was thinking about the hole in the right ventricle of Murray Mortenson's heart, and about Todd's plans to profit from their "video gold." It was raining outside. The rain was washing away the smog. Dave took a deep breath. He felt water on his face. It felt good. His stride lengthened, and his pace quickened as his legs found purpose.

In the corner of Todd's Lair there was a window that his parents believed to be painted shut, but that Todd had patiently freed with an exacto knife over a period of three weeks.

It was perfect for sneaking in and out of.

Dave knew what he had to do.

part two: the stories

THE SOOTHER

IRMA UNFASTENED THE plastic clip on her nursing bra and brought a hard brown nipple to Lucas's mouth. He latched on and sucked greedily. She watched his hands curl into fists. "There," she said, "there there…" Irma rubbed the centre of his back with a soft circular motion. She stroked his forehead and the wisps of fine hair around his ears. He gurgled with contentment. "You're a hungry boy, aren't you? Yes, you are."

The windup mobile turned slowly above their heads. Lucas focused dreamily on the blue geese as they orbited the smiling plastic sun. Music played—tinkling, halting—like Satie on toy piano. His eyes closed all the way. "Shhh," Irma whispered. "Shhhh."

She fed him for the usual twenty minutes, burped him and checked his diaper. "Ooh, somebody needs a change, don't they? Yes, they do!" She moistened a soother in her mouth, then slipped the plastic nubbin to Lucas. She opened his diaper, lifted the legs as best she could, and slid it out from under him. It was dry. "Did mugwamps go pee-pee?" She blew a raspberry into the folds of flesh where double chin met neck. Lucas shrieked with pleasure, kicked his fat legs in the air.

"Okay, enough of that." She maneuvered him onto his belly, smoothed ointment on his bottom, and dusted it with talcum powder. Then she rolled him back onto a clean nappy and did it up nice and snug.

"So, my darling, what will it be? *Funny Bunny* or *Oodles of Poodles*? Let's see...how about poodles today?" Irma opened the book and began to read. "Oodles of poodles in puddles of noodles." She turned the thick cardboard page. "Lambs pushing prams full of apples and yams." She read the remaining eight pages, then closed the book. She checked her watch. It was seven minutes to one. "Okay," she said, standing up, "that's all for today, sweet-cheeks." She kissed his tummy and slipped out of the room.

Lucas sighed. His hour with Irma was the fastest in the week. He lay there for a full minute before sitting up to remove his diaper, which he used to swab the powder and ointment off his buttocks. He lifted the lid on the tickle trunk, retrieved shoes, socks, watch, pinky ring, and his carefully laid-out suit. He dressed quickly, then picked up one of the small white envelopes that said "To:" and "From:" on it. *To: Irma*, he wrote, *From: Baby Luke*. He put two hundred-dollar bills into the envelope and popped it through the slot on the wooden lockbox. He exited through the back door. Irma had things set up nicely. Very private.

He was all the way at the bottom of the rear stairwell before he realized he still had the binky in his mouth. "Shit," he said, pulling it out. He looked up at the stairs. Most likely it would just be Irma in there, cleaning up, preparing for the next client. But what if it weren't? He decided not to risk it. He would bring it along next Tuesday. It was his anyway—that is, assigned to him—and he didn't want to hike two flights again. Not with the irregular heartbeats he'd been having lately. Not with the chest pains.

Lucas stepped into the blaze of day and lit a cigarette.

TRAFFIC WAS BAD. It occurred to Lucas that rush hour was an outdated concept. In Toronto, any hour between 8:00 a.m. and 7:00 p.m. qualified. He checked his cellphone. In the short hour he'd been incommunicado he'd received five messages.

His eldest daughter's voice clanged in his ear: "So, this fucking asshole is refusing to give us our money back, and now he's saying we're going to have to pay for the whole wedding!" No build-up. Instantly frantic. Lucas curbed an impulse to pitch the phone out the window. "I told him about Mom, but he just kept going on about the frickin' contract. So can you do me a favour and call him? Please? I'm totally swamped and stressed, and if we don't get that money back, I don't know what we're going to do. OK, call me once you've talked to him. His name is John Khodabux. *John Kho-da-bux.* I don't have the number handy, but he's the general manager. OK. Call me once you've spoken to him." No goodbye, just a click. The next message was from Megan, his youngest. She rarely used to telephone, but now that she was single and pregnant and finding it difficult to prepare for a child on the small sums she sporadically received from various arts councils—Lucas wasn't exactly sure how it worked—she telephoned often.

"Hi, it's Megan. Sorry to bug you. I called the office and they said you were out for a couple of hours, so I thought I'd try you

on the cell. Um, I don't know if you're going to be in the vicinity
in the near future, but if you are, I was wondering if you could
pop in for ten minutes and help me install the air conditioner.
It's obscenely hot in here, and I'm not supposed to overheat
now. Anyway, you're probably running around doing some
wedding thing for Kate." Did he detect a trace of bitterness in
that? "But if you have a sec, give me a call. If not, I guess I can try
to do it myself." There it was—the threat of self-destruction
that so often accompanied Megan's requests for aid. Only now
his unborn grandchild was the principal figure in jeopardy. He
called her back before listening to the remaining messages.

"Hello?"

"How are you feeling, sweetie?"

"Exhausted, as usual. And it's stinking hot in here."

"Well, I don't want you lifting that air conditioner, okay?"

"Yeah, but I don't know how long I can last in this heat. It's
like a steam bath in here."

"Why don't you get out? See a movie or something."

Megan laughed. "You know how much movies cost these
days? It's like, thirteen bucks or something stupid. Not to
mention the five bucks to get there and back."

"I can giv—"

"Anyway, I don't have the energy."

"Look, I have to meet Uncle Andrew for lunch, but I'll
swing by after, okay?"

"Another invention?"

"I suspect."

"Yikes. Where are you meeting him?"

"Phipps."

"Is there a drugstore around there by any chance?"

"Why, what do you need?"

"I'm supposed to get an iron supplement called ferrous gluconate. Apparently, my iron is really low, which is why I'm so tired."

"What's it called?"

"*Ferr-ous glu-con-ate*. And if you could bring some ice cream? Anything but chocolate or strawberry."

"Vanilla?"

"Um…"

"How about butterscotch?"

"Yeah, I guess."

"OK, I'll—"

"Or if they have Gelato Fresco—the hazelnut. Or the mango-vanilla."

"All right—"

"But not the plain mango, 'cause—"

"Oh, I have another call. Hold on." Lucas checked the display. "It's your mother. I gotta go."

"OK. Not the plain mango. See you soon."

"See you. Hello?" Lucas lit a cigarette.

"It's me. Where are you?"

"On my way to meet Andrew. What's up?"

"You're meeting Andrew?"

"Just for lunch."

"Oh that's rich. Listen, Lucas, we're racking up enough debt with the wedding. Did you know the flowers alone are going to be close to ten thousand dollars?"

"Jesus Christ, are you kidding me?"

"And now this Khoda—whatever the hell his name is, is saying we're going to have to pay for everything."

"I know, I got a message from Kate. *Oh shit.*"

"What's wrong?"

Lucas felt a familiar constriction in his chest, accompanied by a burn in the solar plexus. "Nothing. I just—nothing."

"Are you OK?"

"I'm fine." Lucas flicked the cigarette out the window. Coughed. The pain subsided, but the tightness remained. "How are you doing?"

"My throat feels funny again. But not too bad overall."

"Good."

"So you'll call the hotel?"

"As soon as I get back to the office."

"And you're home this evening, right?"

"Why?"

"The student I hired to do the neighbour's lawn didn't show up again."

"Great. Well, can't you hire someone else?"

"I'm sorry, sweets. I called five places. No one could come until Sunday. I promised we'd have it done by Friday at the absolute latest. You know, they're going to get fed up, and then they're going to spray, and then I'm going to be back in the hospital."

"All right, I'll deal with it," Lucas said.

"It's not that bad. Maybe twenty dandelions."

"Fine. I'll do it after dinner."

"Speaking of which, could you pop by Whole Foods on your way home and pick up some organic quinoa?

"If I have time. It's starting to look like I won't though."

"I would do it, but I have to help Kate buy more bridal party gifts." His wife sighed.

"If I have time I'll get it. Anyway, I'm just pulling up…"

"All right. Don't let him sucker you. I'll see you later."

"Bye." Lucas checked the remaining messages. They were all from work. He called in, dealt quickly with the crisis at hand, then turned off the ringer on his telephone.

"CARPET TILES."

Lucas stared across the table at his brother, Andrew, who was smiling like a conspirator. His eyes were shining. There were cake crumbs in his beard and a chocolate icing smudge on his dress shirt.

"One square foot each—to begin with, anyway. It's like a do-it-yourself area rug. You get me?"

"Um—"

"Say you're living in an apartment, and you want a rug that's four by six. OK, you buy twenty-four carpet tiles, maybe twelve beige and twelve cream, and you put them together in the pattern you desire—like a checkerboard, if you want. Say you move into a house someday. Now you need an area rug that's nine by twelve. No problem, you just buy more carpet tiles and add them on. Maybe you want some chocolate brown in the mix. Fine, you buy a dozen in brown, and get creative with the pattern. You see what I'm saying?" Andrew forked a chunk of cake into his mouth.

"How do they stay together?"

"A patented Velcro-like system."

"You have a patent?"

"Not yet. I have to make the prototype first. But the fastening system isn't the beautiful part; the *concept* is the beautiful part, don't you think? I mean, tell me this isn't a beautiful idea."

"It's not bad."

Andrew waved his fork. "Oh, I forgot the best part! Say Rover or Grandpa loses bladder control in the middle of the rug. Not a problem. You just buy a couple replacement tiles and chuck the offending stains into the garbage. Is that brilliant or what?"

"It's actually a pretty good idea, Andrew." Lucas was surprised. His brother had concocted countless "brilliant" ideas over the years— everything from a hot dog vending machine to a home polygraph test. Only once before had one seemed clever and potentially viable—the spouted paint can, "For clean and easy pouring." Lucas had funded that one to the tune of five thousand dollars. It worked well, but nothing ever came of it. The industry didn't want to mess with the standard. And his brother overlooked the fact that manufacturers wanted their cans to spill. They sold more paint that way.

"Well, I'm gratified," Andrew said. "The man who hates all my ideas likes this one. It must be good."

"I don't hate all your ideas."

"Everything but the paint can."

"That's not true. I've supported many other projects of y—"

"OK, you don't have to rub it in." Andrew pulled out a package of cigarettes. He withdrew one and placed it between his lips. "Got a light?"

"What are you doing? You can't smoke in here."

Andrew sighed and took the cigarette out of his mouth.

"You can't even smoke in bars. What makes you think you can smoke in a cafe?"

"OK, fine. Relax." Andrew rolled his eyes and stuffed the cigarette back into the pack, as if Lucas were personally responsible for the smoking bylaw.

Lucas had an impulse to reach across the table and seize his brother by the throat. "I have a couple cartons for you in the trunk," he said.

"Great. What kind?"

"The usual." Lucas worked for a large tobacco company. He was a manager in the marketing department. His middle child, Leo, despised him for it. On the rare occasions when they hooked up for lunch or coffee, his son insisted on paying for himself. He didn't want a dime of Lucas's "dirty cancer money." Even though Leo was generally joyless, and seldom pleasant to be around, Lucas had to give him credit for acting in ways that supported his copious convictions. Megan and Kate, on the other hand, frequently berated him for his work but seemed content to benefit from the proceeds of tobacco sales.

Andrew pushed his plate away. "You want to step out for a smoke?"

"Yeah. I have to go anyway. I have to drop by Megan's place on the way to the office."

"How's she doing?"

"She's fine. Tired."

"I can't really see Meggie as a mom, for some reason."

"Oh, she'll take to it, I think," Lucas said, trying to mask his uncertainty. He stood and carried both trays to the counter.

His brother followed. As soon as they were out of the café, they lit cigarettes.

"Car's just up here. Why don't we go get the smokes?"

"Cool," said Andrew.

As they walked in silence, Lucas could feel the hamster wheel turning in his brother's head.

So, Lukey," he said as they got to the Lexus. "How'd you like to save my life, and partner with me on this carpet tile venture?"

"JOHN KHADABOX, PLEASE."

"That's *Khodabux*. I'll put you through now."

"*Dad!*"

"One sec, Megan."

"John Khodabux's office, can I help you?"

"I'd like to speak to Mr. Khodabux, please."

"May I ask who's calling?"

"Lucas Monahan."

"One moment please."

Lucas watched his daughter unpack the drugstore items he had purchased, the ferrous gluconate and ice cream, also some extra items she figured she could use: toilet paper, Kleenex, dry roasted peanuts, Wrigley's Spearmint gum, a *Vanity Fair* magazine. He thought she'd be pleased, but something was wrong. She looked angry. There were tears swelling in her eyes.

"John Khodabux speaking."

"Yes, this is Lucas Monahan calling with regard to the Kate Monahan–Jeremy Fish wedding."

"Yes, sir. What can I do for you today?"

"Well, what you could do, sir, is keep our initial three-thousand-dollar deposit, refund the rest of our money, and call it a day."

"I'm sorry, sir. I'm afraid I can't do that. But I would be happy to provide you with a copy of the contract—"

"Forget the contract, OK? The contract doesn't take into account my wife's debilitating condition, does it? A condition that was diagnosed long after my daughter booked the ballroom at your hotel." He saw Megan roll her eyes. She didn't believe her mother was genuinely ill. "Don't you think a mother should be able to attend her own daughter's wedding?"

"Of course, sir."

"Well, my wife won't be able to attend our daughter's wedding without getting sick from the pesticides sprayed in your kitchen and ballrooms."

"We don't spray in the ballrooms, sir."

"You spray in the adjoining kitchen, do you not?"

"Yes, sir."

"And in the guest rooms."

"Very rarely, yes."

"And on the grounds? In the outdoor areas, on the grass?"

"Of course."

"Well, my wife is extremely sensitive. There's no way we can have the wedding there."

"I understand, sir. And I apologize for the inconvenience. Of course, you're free to hold the wedding wherever you wish."

"I realize that. But if you're holding us to the full cost of the event, we won't be able to have it anywhere but City Hall or perhaps our backyard. Are you saying, given the extenuating circumstances, that you still refuse?"

"I apologize, sir, but this is why we have contracts. Your daughter booked the room more than a year ago. The catering department has finalized the menu, arranged for staff…It's too late now for us to use that room. Had your daughter cancelled more than thirty days before the event, perhaps we could have done things differently."

Lucas could feel his blood pressure rising. He had a vision of driving fast to the luxury hotel and placing a gun in John Khodabux's mouth. Instead, he said calmly, "Well, that's very inflexible of you. So here's what I'm going to do. I'm going to write you a cheque for—what is it, thirty-two thousand dollars?"

"Roughly, sir. Thirty-two thousand, seven hundred, and eighty-four remaining on the balance."

"Fine. I'm going to write you that cheque. Then I'm going to write a letter to Mr. Samuel Black, the chairman and founder of your hotel chain. In that missive, I'm going to explain my wife's condition, and how my daughter's wedding was totally ruined by your hotel, well, *you* specifically. I'm also going to send Mr. Black photocopies of the letters I have written to all the local and national newspapers about this sad affair. I have a friend at the *Toronto Sun* who specializes in this kind of story— you know: the little guy getting screwed by the unfeeling corporation. Maybe I'll ask him to run a photo of my daughter in her wedding dress, and my wife in her wheelchair, looking sad in front of your hotel. What do you think? Would that be good for business, or your career?"

Silence. A small puff of exhaled air. "All right, sir. I think I see your point."

"Oh good. That's good. Thank you for being so understanding. Now, how do we resolve this?"

"We can forego the remaining balance, and simply keep the money deposited—"

"No, no, no, no. We've already paid for forty percent of the wedding. That's ridiculous. No. I'm prepared to forfeit the three thousand dollars initially deposited, but that's it. End of story." Lucas waited. He could hear the general manager breathing on the other end of the phone. After what seemed like an unnaturally long interval, he spoke.

"All right, Mr. Monahan. If your daughter would like to get in touch with me, we can make arrangements to refund the most recent deposit."

"That's great. Thank you very much. Listen, why don't you keep an extra five hundred and buy yourself a nice bottle of Scotch."

"It's not necessary, sir."

"Well, I'll leave it up to you. Thank you kindly for your time, Mr. Khodabux."

"No problem, sir."

Lucas hung up the phone, feeling smug and triumphant, but his daughter's sour face made the fizz of success evaporate.

"Wheelchair?" she said.

"So I embellished a little." Lucas laughed.

Megan did not laugh.

"What's wrong, sweetie?"

"Well…no, it's nothing."

"What? What's the matter?"

"Look, I appreciate you bringing me stuff, I mean, I didn't even ask for half of this, but the thing I *did* ask you to get is wrong." Megan looked as if she was going to cry. "I specifically said *not* to get the plain mango. I don't like the plain mango."

"You said mango-vanilla."

"Yeah, together—mango and vanilla swirled together."

"I know. I looked for it, but they didn't have it, honey. So I got mango and I got vanilla and I figured you could mix them yourself."

"Whatever. It doesn't matter."

"It's exactly the same thing. Except this way you get twice as much."

"Fine. It doesn't matter."

"Honey—"

"Let's just do the air conditioner."

"All right."

Megan's bedroom was small and cluttered and smelled unfresh. There was a futon on the floor, covered in threadbare burgundy sheets and a crumpled beige duvet that had numerous stains and cigarette burns. Next to the bed was the new crib. Blond wood with crisp white sheets, a pretty gingham bumper in apple-green, and a Winnie the Pooh mobile. Lucas found the contrast touching and a little sad.

"I think you should move," he said.

"Oh please, don't start." Megan tensed. "I'm not in any shape to start packing and hauling boxes."

"You wouldn't have to haul boxes. I'd hire a mover."

"Dad, I don't even have the energy to do laundry, let alone pack up this place!"

"All right. Forget it."

"I can move in a year, when the baby is old enough to give a shit one way or another. And anyway, I don't want to over-prepare, just in case something happens."

"Like what?"

"I don't know. Not every birth is successful."

"Well, yours will be."

"I hope so. But it's not unheard of for women to die in childbirth, even in big-city hospitals."

"Meggie, you'll be fine, I promise. And so will the baby." Lucas reached out to touch his daughter's belly, but she pulled away.

"Sorry, I just—I don't see why people think they can just touch my stomach all of a sudden."

"I'm not 'people'; I'm your father."

"Anyway...I don't like it."

"Fine." Lucas surveyed the ancient air conditioner sitting on the floor below the window. "Are you sure this thing still works?"

"I think so. Yeah."

"Get me a cloth. I'll clean it up a bit."

Lucas scoured the grime off the air conditioner and then vacuumed out the dust. It took him close to half an hour, and even without his jacket and tie, he was sweating heavily. "OK," he said, "let's get this sucker in." He bent down to lift the thing.

"Wait," Megan said. "You have to build a platform first. The window's too tall for the air conditioner."

"Oh."

"Here." She handed him a plastic bag full of bits of wood—small chunks of two by four and one by three. "Ryan used these."

"This seems kind of flimsy...Do you have a tape measure?"

"Ryan took it."

Lucas emptied the bag onto the floor. He selected a couple of similarly sized pieces of wood and began assembling a platform on the windowsill.

Megan sat on the futon and watched. "I can't believe Mom almost cost you thirty-two thousand dollars."

"More than that," Lucas said.

"It's all in her head, you know."

Lucas didn't know, but he wondered. His wife's environmental sensitivities had flared up shortly after the violent death of her long-time lover—a depressive Czech who hanged himself—and had been worsening ever since. "Whether it's psychosomatic or not is completely irrelevant. Your mother isn't feeling well, and you should have empathy for her. She's had a tough year."

"Helping plan Kate's wedding is so tough?"

"I'm talking about one of her closest friends passing away."

Megan didn't respond, and Lucas couldn't tell if she knew that Josef had been more than a friend to her mother. He was certain, however, that nobody knew that *he* knew they had been more than friends, meeting once, sometimes twice a week at the Intercontinental Hotel on Bloor Street. Lucas had hired a private detective to confirm his suspicions. Not that he wanted to confront his wife. No. He just wanted to know why she was suddenly looking so well and feeling so breezy and at the same time having frequent, guilt-induced nightmares. He'd thought about reassuring her, telling her that he knew, and that it was all right, but ultimately decided against it. He didn't want to rob her affair of its illicit allure. Franny had always been a devotee of anything European, particularly French—perfume, fashion, cinema, sensibility. She had a collection of Hermes scarves, for example, which she treasured and wore often. She loved Chanel and Dior. When they went out for a nice dinner, they went to a French restaurant. When they went on vacation, they went to Paris or Provence. Franny spoke French fairly well. She could tell a good croissant from a bad one. Lucas presumed that having a lover on the side, a Czech lover at that, made Franny feel sophisticated and a little less like a suburban Canadian housewife. She started to take an interest in the world again. She bought season tickets to the symphony. She joined the Art Gallery of Ontario. She drove downtown and stood in line for hours to see subtitled movies at the Toronto International Film Festival. She was vital again, very much like the young woman he'd wooed and married. Then the melancholy Czech went and offed himself (seemingly, because he had written a twelve-hundred-page novel that thirty-seven consecutive editors had declined to publish). Now Franny hid in the house most of the time, worrying about the ways in which the environment—everything from power lines to perfume— could be depriving her of health and happiness. It was tragic.

And there was nothing Lucas could do except try to be compassionate and understanding when she began evicting everything in their home that wasn't 100 percent cotton or natural, including recently installed wall-to-wall carpeting, and half their furnishings, or when she had her "attacks"—almost every time they tried to go out for dinner or to see a movie. They never travelled any more. Airplanes made Franny sick. So did trains and boats, and long automobile rides. She didn't dye her hair any more. She no longer wore makeup. Lucas thought she was still beautiful. He loved his wife.

"OK," Lucas said, eyeballing the space in the window. "Let's see if this works."

"It worked last year," Megan said. "Do you want help lifting?"

"I don't want you lifting anything, sweetie." Lucas bent at the knees and got a hold of the air conditioner. He managed to hoist it up and prop it on the edge of the makeshift platform, but as he tried to slide it into place, pieces of wood began to move forward underneath it, and just as his brain processed the fact that the platform was actually too low, leaving a large gap at the top of the box, gravity and poor planning sucked the teetering metal box from his grasp and sent it plummeting to earth.

"FUCK!"

"Dad!" Megan emitted a cross between a gasp and a scream and then proceeded to sob vigorously.

Lucas leaned out the second-storey window. The air conditioner had landed on the lawn, crushing nothing more important than the ironic garden gnomes of the ironic film students who rented the flat on the main floor. Lucas's fear turned instantly to rage. He had an impulse to put his fist through the glass, but a sharp burn behind the solar plexus caused him to sink back onto the futon and take deep breaths in through the nose and out through the mouth. His heart was skipping beats. He had to cough a few times to regulate it. "All right," he said, tamping down his anger. "It's OK. Nobody got hurt, and that thing was a piece of crap anyway. I'm going to get you a new one, OK, sweetie?"

"What, now?" Megan wiped a blob of snot from her nose.

"Yeah. Right now." Lucas comforted his daughter, who was still crying a little. She allowed him to embrace her for a couple of seconds, but then pulled away, saying, "You stink like cigarettes."

Lucas took out his wallet and removed two twenties. "Here," he said, placing them on the dresser. "Give this to the people downstairs when you see them."

ON HIS WAY TO the Home Depot, Lucas checked his messages. There was one from Kate, wanting to know if he had called the hotel. Another from his wife, wanting to know the same thing. And there was one from his boss, Jane, wondering when he planned to mosey on back to the office. That was the word she used: *mosey*. Rather snide, he thought, for someone who invariably relied on him to solve every problem in the office. He called her back, but she was on another line. He left a message saying that he'd had a family emergency he had to deal with, and that he would try to make it back as soon as possible. Lucas checked his watch; it was already 4:03. He added that there was a chance that he may

not make it in today, but that he'd be there early the following morning—by 6:30 a.m. at the latest—and that he could
now be reached on his cellphone if need be. He turned the
ringer back on and called Kate to fill her in about the hotel.
Franny was with her, buying bridal party gifts, so he didn't
have to phone his wife with the news. Lucas then called
Andrew and asked him to meet him at the hardware store.
He figured since he'd just pledged three thousand dollars to
his Carpet Tile pipedream, he could ask his brother to ferry
the new air conditioner to Megan's and install it. His brother,
who claimed to have just had a manicure, somewhat grudg-
ingly agreed. Still, by the time Lucas picked out and paid for
the air conditioner and a suitable piece of lumber on which
to prop the thing, it was five o'clock. He would not be returning to the office. He would however, have just enough time
to boot it to Whole Foods, grab some organic quinoa, and
make it home by the expected hour—six o'clock or shortly
thereafter.

Lucas deked and darted the Lexus through the rush hour
crush. He was standing in line at the store when his cellphone
rang. The number on the display was unfamiliar, but he
answered just in case it was his wife calling from somewhere
other than home.

"Hello?"

"Hey, Dad, it's me."

"Hey, Leo, how are you doing? Long time no blab." Lucas
handed the quinoa to the cashier, who placed it on the scale
and weighed it.

"Yeah. That's true…Um, actually, Dad, I'm not doing so good."

"Why, what's wrong?"

"$7.48," said the cashier. Lucas handed her a twenty.

"Well…it's kind of a long story. The thing is, are you free right now?"

"Why, what's going on?"

"Well, I sort of need you to come to the police station on Dundas Street, um, 255 Dundas West. Otherwise they're gonna keep me here all night."

"Keep you for what? Are you OK?"

"I'm fine. It's just—I've been assaulted and arrested and I need you to come get me out of here."

LUCAS CALLED HIS WIFE and told her that he had a work emergency to deal with. He did not tell her that their son, the pacifist, had been arrested and charged with assault causing bodily harm. Apparently, Leo had tackled an undercover security guard on Yonge Street, just outside of Consumers Drug Mart. He scuffled with the guard—who had been trying to get Leo's girlfriend, Perdita, to return to the store office with the nail polish she'd just slipped into her pocket without paying—and inadvertently broke his thumb. Lucas was able to convince the police to release his son, pledging to escort him to his appearance before a Justice of the Peace the following morning at 9:00 a.m. So much for getting to the office by 6:30. Jane was not going to be happy. There would be words.

Lucas lit a cigarette as they exited the station.

"Look, Dad, I just want you to know, it wasn't my fault. That fascist fuck assaulted Perdita."

"What do you mean 'assaulted'?"

"We're walking out the door, and all of a sudden this fuckin' skinhead gorilla is all over her, grabbing her arm, trying to yank her back in."

"Yeah, well...she stole from the store."

"Why, 'cause she's black?"

"Nooo. Because she's a thief."

"Perdita is not a thief."

"Fine. Because she wanted free nail polish."

"Uch! She just put it there 'cause her hands were full of stuff—stuff that we bought! She didn't want to drop it. Believe me, Perdita can afford all the nail polish she wants. She has a very good job. She just forgot about it 'cause we were debating something on our way out."

"Uh huh."

"God, you're such a racist!"

"I'm not a racist, Leo." Lucas sighed and flicked away his cigarette. "I'm sure Perdita is very nice. Are you bringing her to the wedding? I'd like to meet her."

"I was going to. But not if everyone's going to think she's a thief."

"I don't think she's a thief, okay. I believe you. And nobody else needs to know...if we're lucky, that is. Shit, Leo, did you have to break the guy's thumb?"

"It was an accident, Dad. I was just trying to keep him off of her. Anyway, that fuckin' animal doesn't need a thumb. It's probably not even opposable."

Lucas tried to smile as he embraced his son. "All right," he said, "I have to go. We'll clear this thing up tomorrow morning. If need be, I have a very good lawyer."

"You're not paying for my lawyer, Dad. I'll get legal aid if I need a lawyer."

Lucas wasn't in the mood to argue about his dirty tobacco money. "Fine," he said. "We can figure it out tomorrow. Do you want a ride home?"

"In the car that cancer and heart disease bought? No thanks. I'll walk."

"I'll see you in the morning then."

"Yeah."

"Don't be late."

"I won't."

"And, Leo…"

"What?"

"Maybe you should take some of the piercings out."

"I'll think about it," Leo said as he walked away.

WHEN LUCAS ARRIVED home, he found his wife stretched out on the sofa with a compress over her eyes and forehead. "Sorry I'm so late," he said. "I got the quinoa."

"What time is it?" she asked, without lifting the compress.

"Almost seven-thirty."

"Oh. I'm sorry, I couldn't make dinner. I don't feel well."

"What's wrong?"

"Oh you know, every store we went into there was someone drenched in perfume, or the rugs had just been cleaned… My head is killing me. I just feel overloaded."

"Do you want something to eat?"

"Thanks, but I couldn't eat with this headache. And my mouth is sore. The mucous membranes again. I think they're reacting to something."

"Well, I'm going to grab a bite. I'm starving."

"Wait," his wife said as he moved toward the kitchen. "You have to do the dandelions while it's still light out."

"Oh shit, I forgot."

Franny sat up. "Please, Lucas. I'm afraid they're going to spray."

Lucas surveyed his wife, small on the big straw-coloured couch across the room. She did look afraid. Her bangs, damp from the washcloth, were sticking straight up. He was reminded of a baby bird surrounded by nest.

"All right," he said. "I'll take care of it."

Lucas changed out of his suit, took a piss, then went to weed the neighbour's lawn. At first he was quite thorough, digging deep to get the absurdly long dandelion roots, but as the light faded and he grew increasingly famished, he began to rake them from the grass with his fingers—which meant he would be back in two weeks to do it again. Luckily, the neighbours spared him the indignity of coming out to watch him on his hands and knees, although he did notice a couple of discreet peeks through the living-room blinds. It was 9:25 and dark when he returned to the house. Franny had gone to bed, but she'd left a note on the kitchen table: Jane called. Wants you to call her at home, up till eleven. P.S. You should probably sleep on the pullout. Don't think I could handle cigarette smell tonight.

Lucas bolted some cheese and crackers, and six or seven fistfuls of cashews. He went down to the basement and made up the pullout couch. The last thing he wanted to do was talk to his boss. Lucas stretched out on the bed and stared at the ceiling fan. He thought about Irma. He thought about the mobile with the blue geese. That's when he remembered the soother.

It was in his jacket pocket. He fished it out and took it to the bathroom to rinse clean. Then he locked the door, turned out the light, and curled up in the tub. Lucas put the binky in his mouth. Very soon he would get up and return Jane's call. But now, for just a moment, Lucas closed his eyes. He thought about the soft music and those blue geese, moving slowly, slowly around the smiling sun.

WONDERFUL

CRYING. THAT WAS the last thing George heard before he left the house. Had he shut the door behind him? He couldn't remember. He felt nothing, not even the cold, though he'd left without a coat. Fat snowflakes stuck to his sweater and hair as he moved toward the centre of town, to the bridge and the falls.

"Merry Christmas, Mr. Bayliss."

One of the Cole children doing something on the lawn. Snowman?

"You all right, Mr. Bayliss?"

George kept walking. He kept walking until he made the Edgewater and his favourite bar stool.

"Hey, George. What are you doing in here on Christmas Eve?"

"The usual, please."

Simon scooped some ice into a glass and poured the Bushmills. "Everything OK?"

"Make it a double."

"Hmm. That doesn't sound so good. On the tab?"

"No." George fished the last twenty out of his wallet and dropped it on the bar. It seemed like the thing to do. All was gone. Might as well complete the picture. "That's fine," said George, moving away from Simon's concerned, inquiring gaze to a table in the corner where he chugged the whisky in three swallows. No burn in the throat. And he was as sober as before. He held his hand over the lit candle in the centre of the table. He thought about Marianne's tears. And the accusations that preceded them. Again, he felt the stab of *How could you?!* The pierce of *Why didn't you?!* Right. Absolutely. How *could* he have let things devolve so disastrously? Why *didn't* he let her know what was going on until it was past repair? He'd been hiding the slide for over two years now, ping-ponging the credit card payments, cashing the RRSPs (even the RESPs) to try to keep the business afloat. He'd pay for things that maintained the illusion of solvent—nice clothes for Marianne and the kids, the cable and phone bills—while neglecting significant vitals, like the mortgage. He was convinced the business would rally. He was convinced of it. He would work hard and fix everything, and Marianne would never ever know how bad it had been. That was the plan. And on occasion it looked as if things might actually be turning around, but in the end…no. It was like trying to build on quicksand—it didn't matter how hard he worked. Now his wife and children would have to leave their home. And he didn't even have first and last for a lousy apartment.

George squeezed the burned flesh on the palm of his hand. *God*, he said in his mind, *I'm not a praying man, but if you're up there and you can hear me, please…show me the way. I'm at the end of my rope.* George waited. He scanned the bar. The Ryan twins were playing darts. A group of teens was playing pool. Everyone else seemed to be involved in the electronic trivia game lighting up the monitors suspended from the ceiling. There was music from the jukebox. A rock 'n' roll version of "Frosty the Snowman." Andrea, the good waitress, stopped at his table.

"Hey, George. Merry Christmas." She placed his empty glass on her tray. "Listen, thanks again for putting in the word with Simon. I don't know how I would've made it through the holidays without this job. You want another? I'm buying."

Before he could answer, the heavily loaded tray slipped from Andrea's hand and spilled onto the table and George.

"Oh, my gosh, I'm so sorry!" She plucked a glass and an ashtray from his lap but hesitated before brushing away ice cubes and cigarette butts.

"It's okay," George said. "Don't worry about it."

"Sorry!"

George got up and walked out of the bar. He walked down the street and across the bridge to the cliff on the north bank of the river, just below the falls. He moved close to the edge and the swirling black water. He stared hard at that swirling black water.

He jumped.

Strangely, as he entered the river he felt nothing, except perhaps a momentary flash of relief. But moments later as his body surfaced, he was seized by a blast of intolerable pain, one that seemed to trigger in each of his cells an overpowering desire to live. George sucked for air, but his lungs felt as if they had been squeezed shut. Myriad confused images of

Marianne, the kids, his brother, and mother cut through his brain as he thrashed in the water, determined to survive. Pure will propelled him toward the edge, and just when he knew he couldn't last another minute in the freeze, his feet found bottom. He would make it.

As George struggled onto the embankment, a stranger appeared out of nowhere—an old man with ruddy cheeks and twinkling eyes and charmingly dishevelled white hair. He kicked George back into the river.

"Help," George screamed. "Please?!"

"I thought you wanted to die?" the man said.

"No. I want to live!" George hoisted himself half out of the water.

The man smiled benevolently and kicked him back in. "Just relax," he said.

"Please! My wife—my children need me!"

The man smiled. "Trust me, George, with an eight-hundred-thousand-dollar life insurance policy, you're worth more to them dead than alive."

"How do you know that?! Who are you?"

"Somebody's dying to meet me," he said to the sky, with an "aw, shucks" chuckle. The man crouched and extended his hand for a shake. "Terrance Angel, the Second. Very pleased to make your acquaintance."

George grabbed his arm and held on with every iota of remaining strength. If he was going down, this lunatic was going with him.

"Oh Georgie," the man said, yanking him onto the bank with one effortless pull. "Why bother?"

George was shivering too violently to speak. Even after Terrance removed his overcoat and draped it around him, he shook and shook. Terrance—now wearing old-fashioned long johns and rubber boots—put his hands on George's shoulders. He felt a tremendous warmth surge through him then, and in less than a minute his shaking had subsided, the pain had flown, and his clothes, inexplicably, had dried.

"There now," Terrance said, helping him to his feet. "Are you sure you don't want to hop back in?" He gestured to the river and patted George on the bum.

"Of course I'm sure!"

"Because if you're worried about Marianne and little Matthew and Zoey, I can assure you they'll be just fine on their own."

"Oh really?"

"Indubitably."

"Look," George said, doffing the madman's coat, "if you knew anything about me, you would know that my wife and children love and depend on me."

"Is that right?"

"As a matter of fact, quite a few people in this town love and depend on me."

"Really?"

"Oh I'm not saying I'm the most important person in the world... but I'm a good man, and I make a difference in people's lives. I make a difference in this community."

Terrance smiled gently. "Well, George, I think you may be exaggerating your impact just a tad. Not only would it not be the end of the world if you drowned yourself in the river tonight, it wouldn't really matter much if you had never been born at all."

George gasped at the old man's audacity. "How dare you," he sputtered.

"It's true," Terrance said. Then looking heavenward, he asked, "May I?" A star gleamed, as if in response. Terrance grinned and took George by the arm. "Come along," he said.

"Don't touch me! You're crazy."

"Crazy. Why, if I'm so crazy, how come your clothes are dry?"

George opened his mouth to answer but no answer arrived.

"You've been given a great gift, George. I'm going to show you what life would be like in Fenton Falls if you had never been born at all." Terrance gripped George's elbow and steered him toward the bridge. "Come along," he said. "Let's get a drink at the Edgewater and warm ourselves up."

"HAPPY HOLIDAYS, GENTLEMEN. What can I get you?" Simon didn't seem at all surprised that George had returned so soon to the bar.

"Glass of milk, please," Terrance said.

"And I'll have another."

"Another…milk?" Simon said.

"No. The usual."

"And that would be?"

"Come off it, Sime, you know very well."

Simon smiled. "Sorry, must be a bit foggy tonight. Refresh my memory."

"What you served me half an hour ago; what you've been serving me practically every weeknight for the past ten—no, more like, twelve years."

Simon looked amused. "Listen, pal, maybe you'd better stick with milk. Or coffee. How about a nice hot cup of coffee?"

"I want a Bushmills on the rocks, and you know it."

Simon moved off and began preparing the drinks.

Terrance said, "Relax, George. He doesn't know you."

"Of course he knows me."

"How can he know you if you've never been born?"

George laughed and shook his head. "Right." But something in Terrance's smile made him pause. He scanned the bar. The Ryan twins were still playing darts. The same group of teens was still playing pool. The monitors still flashed their trivia. Bad Christmas music continued to issue from the jukebox.

"Cheers," Simon said, placing their drinks on the bar. "That'll be $6.75."

"On the tab, please." George lifted his glass and sipped.

"And what tab would that be?"

"My tab."

Simon's amiable expression morphed into something less benign.

"George Bayliss's tab—you know, *George Bayliss*, the guy who approved the loan that allowed you to buy this establishment in the first place. The guy who gave you a ten-dollar tip a half-hour ago."

Simon sighed. "Okay, you know what, pal, I don't know what you're on about, but I'm really not in the mood. That's $6.75, okay."

George knew he had spent his last twenty, but thought perhaps he could squeak $6.75 onto one of his beleaguered credit cards. He reached for his wallet, but there was no wallet. His pant pockets were empty.

"I must have lost my wallet in the river," said George.

Simon folded his arms across his chest.

"Do me a favour and pay for this round, Terrance."

"Oh I don't have any cash." Terrance giggled, a milk moustache shining atop his lip. "Angels don't carry money, you know."

"OK, that's it—" Simon leaned forward on the bar.

"Wait," George interrupted, "get Andrea. Andrea offered to buy me a drink earlier."

"Andrea? Andrea who?" Simon asked.

"Andrea Sloane."

"Andrea Sloane's not here," Simon said, looking around the bar.

"What are you talking about? She's here. She was my waitress a half-hour ago…"

"Okay, Merry Christmas. Drinks on the house, boys, but I'd like you to finish up quick. You get me?"

"I tell you Andrea Sloane is working tonight!"

"Andrea Sloane doesn't work here, pal. She's never worked here. Okay? Goodnight." Simon snatched up their glasses and emptied them into the sink.

"Much obliged," Terrance said, wiping his mouth with his sleeve. "A Merry Christmas to you, sir." He slid off his barstool and took George by the arm. "Come along, George."

"But I just saw her. She spilled a tray of drinks on me. She thanked me for getting her this job!"

Terrance pushed George toward the exit. He manoeuvred him out the door and onto the snowy street. "No, George, you didn't help Andrea Sloane get a job. How could you recommend her for a job if you had never been born?"

George stared at Terrance. "But she just said—Oh, I'm confused. I could've sworn she just said…"

"What, George?"

"That she didn't know how she would've made it through the holidays without that job. She has a son, you know. He's five."

"I guess we'd better check on her then. Since you weren't alive to get her that job, she must be in a bit of pickle, eh? Come on…" Terrance led George up the street and around the corner to Mercer's Department Store. He tapped on the glass picture window. "Have a gander."

George peered through spray-on snow, past the Xbox display to the cash counter where Andrea was ringing up a teddy bear dressed in a Santa Claus suit. She looked different than she had in the bar. Her hair was now in braids. And she was wearing a green sweater instead of a red jersey.

"That's weird," George said as he wandered to the entrance and into the store. "Andrea."

She looked up.

"You work here now?"

"Um, yeah. Do we know each other?"

"You don't know me?" George said, approaching the counter.

She smiled, confused. "Sorry. Should I?"

"You don't know me? George Bayliss?"

"Oh," said Andrea, handing her customer a credit card slip to sign. "Are you related to Harvey Bayliss?"

"Of course. He's my brother."

"One sec," Andrea said, completing the transaction. "Merry Christmas!" She handed the bagged bear to the customer and turned to George. "I didn't know Mr. Bayliss had a brother. I guess you must be in town for the holidays?"

"I guess…"

"Hey, where you going? Are you all right?"

George stumbled blindly out of the store and slumped on the bench where Terrance was seated, head back, mouth open, catching snowflakes on his tongue.

"This is crazy," said George, his heart hammering. "I don't understand."

"It's really very simple, George. You weren't there to put in a word to Simon about Andrea, so she had to keep trying to find work. That's how she landed the job at Mercer's. She doesn't know it yet, but she'll be managing the place someday."

"Oh."

"And because they close in half an hour, Andrea won't be toiling all night in a smoky bar. She'll be able to spend Christmas Eve at home with little Timmy."

George sat on the bench and took it all in. He took it all in and said, "Okay. Fine. Maybe I didn't have such a big impact on Andrea Sloane's life. But she said she knew my brother, Harvey."

"So?"

"So, my brother wouldn't be alive today if weren't for me."

"Is that right?"

"Yes. That's right. When we were kids we went tob—"

"Tobogganing. I know." Terrance stood up and began walking toward the park. "And Harvey's Snow Warrior went out of control, and he slid onto the river, and went through the ice, and you sped down the hill, and inched your way out, and lay down on your belly, and blah blah blah blah blah." Terrance said it as if it were a boring speech he'd been forced to recite every morning for ten years.

"And let's not forget," George said, trailing behind, "Harvey's practically a hero in this town. He saved the life of a pregnant woman who was in a car accident! Pulled her right out of a burning automobile and rushed her to the hospital in his car. He saved two lives that day, which means I saved three, if you think about it."

"Well, George, that's not entirely accurate." Terrance pointed to a steep hill at the south end of the park in which they now stood. "Shall we go back to that supposedly fateful day?"

Before George could answer, Terrance waved his hands, and in a flash they were standing at the base of the tobogganing hill. But now it was day. The sun was shining, making the snow sparkle. Dogs were barking and children were moving up and down the hill. George recognized his peers from long ago. There was little Daphne Floros and James Luscombe and Daryl Samotowka and Davey Whitton. And there was his future wife, Marianne Cunningham, so cute in her pink parka and woolly white cap. George's heart surged with joy and nostalgia. "This is incredible!" he shouted, running up the slope, dodging toboggans, and laughing. "Where am I?" he said. "I don't see me."

"You were never born, George."

"Oh. Right. Well, where's Harvey?"

"He's not here," Terrance said. "Harvey's at home, watching television. Remember? It was your idea to go tobogganing that day. Harvey wanted to stay home and watch cartoons."

"I don't recall."

"If you'd never been born, Harvey wouldn't have ended up in the river in the first place."

"Oh." George stopped to catch his breath. "So, he'd still be around to rescue that pregnant woman when the time came?"

"Right. But it's not such a good thing, George, truth be told."

"How can you say that!?"

Terrance waved his hands and they were alone again in the dark park. "That woman's son is going to grow up to be trouble, George. A pack of trouble. He's going to sexually assault more than a dozen women, and kill two of them before he's caught."

"No!"

"Yes. I'm afraid so. Now, had you been born and *failed* to save your brother, that would've made quite an impact on a number of lives."

"Oh my gosh." George sighed. He was silent for a long while, then said, "But wait a minute; what about all my civic actions? I've been very involved in community affairs. You know, I organized and led the 'Be Nice, Clear Your Ice' campaign. Who knows who might have slipped and killed themselves if it weren't for me?"

"*I* know, actually. Nobody would've slipped."

"Well, what about the Ride-A-Thon I put together? We raised funds to erect a statue of our town's founder."

"Didn't think you'd inquire about that one. Okay. Let's check it out."

George followed Terrance to the lighted south entrance of the park where the bust of William Fenton III should have been sitting.

"Ah-ha! Not here, is it? Just this puny little plaque that's been here forever."

Terrance gave George a pity smile. "Well, you got me there. It's true. If you had never been born, that chunk of bronze would not exist."

"I admit it's not much," George said, suddenly sheepish.

"Especially since the artist you commissioned did a terrible job. Looked as if Fenton himself had been made of bronze, if you know what I mean."

"I'm not really an expert." George chewed a hangnail. "But you know what? It's not about the art, it's about the *pride*."

"Okay."

"And anyway," he said, following Terrance out of the park, "there are other things I've done. Truly worthwhile things."

"I'm all ears, Georgie."

"Well, what about my mom? I've been giving her three hundred and twenty dollars a month for the past five years. Without me—"

"She had only one child to raise, and was able to sock away some dough for her golden years," said Terrance.

"Oh. Hmm. Okay. Well, what about all the risky loans I've approved for people in this town? All the opportunities I've created and dreams I've fulfilled?"

"Without you around to do so, the Morton family took over the Savings and Loan. Heidi Morton does your job."

"Really? Heidi Morton."

"Turns out she's just as nutty and generous as you when it comes to doling out the cashola. But unlike you, when the bank founders, she has a wealthy father to step in and personally save her and the company."

"I see."

"Are you all right, George?"

"Yeah, I'm just—I feel a bit dizzy."

"Do you want to sit down?"

"No." George took a couple of big breaths. "No, sitting down is not what I want to do."

"Hey, wait up! Where are you going?"

"Home," George called out.

"But you don't have a home!"

George jogged down Wellington Street. He sped up and turned right on Croft, then left on Pineway until he stood, panting, in front of his house—number seventy-two. Terrance was waiting on the porch when he arrived.

"Listen, George. Before you—"

"Does Marianne still live here?" The house looked the same, except for a more elaborate Christmas display, which included a rooftop Santa and sleigh complete with illuminated reindeers that appeared to have just lifted off the shingles and taken flight.

"Yes," Terrance said. "Marianne always loved this drafty old house. But wait." He caught George's wrist before he could ring the bell. "I'd better show you something first." Terrance waved his hand, and in a flash he and George were standing in the living room of number seventy-two Pineway. "Don't worry," he said. "I've made it so that they can't see or hear us."

Two children were watching television and eating a chocolate orange. The house smelled deliciously of roast turkey and balsam fir.

A small cry of longing and love escaped from George's throat as he advanced toward Matthew and Zoey. Then he stopped cold, transfixed and horrified, trying to process what he was seeing.

"Is that the one what stole Christmas?" said the girl who looked a lot like Zoey but wasn't Zoey. Her lips were smeared with chocolate.

"Yup," said the boy who looked a lot like Matthew but wasn't Matthew.

A wave of numb panic swept over George as he stared at the children who weren't quite his children. Like Matthew and Zoey, they had green eyes and ginger hair—corkscrew curls cascading—but they were considerably skinnier and their rounded faces had become oval. All of their features looked bizarrely elongated. It was like seeing the reflection of his progeny in a funhouse mirror.

"This is extremely disturbing," croaked George, his mouth dry and sticky. "Where's Marianne?"

"Upstairs. But you might not want to—"

George bounded up the stairs to the bedroom, where he found Marianne seated cross-legged on the bed, watching her favourite decorating show on television. And seated behind her, also watching the show—something George had long refused to do—was Dennis Cole. He was massaging Marianne's shoulders.

"Oh my God!" said George. "I don't believe this!"

"That's good there," said Marianne as Dennis Cole probed the muscles of her back with a strong thumb.

"I can't fucking believe this!"

"Why not?" said Terrance. "Dennis Cole is a very nice guy and, as it happens, a good father, and a fine husband to Marianne."

"Yeah, I know he's a *nice guy*, he's my neighbour, or at least he was my neighbour. I just—HE DOESN'T BELONG HERE." George lunged at Dennis Cole's fingers—he would tear them from his wife's back!—but his own hands were completely insubstantial, like a ghost's, unable to grab or grip anything in this alternate world, unable to stop Dennis Cole from caressing the slim, downy neck of his beloved Marianne.

"No!" moaned George. "This can't be…"

"Come, come," said Terrance. "Is it really so shocking that Marianne would end up with Dennis Cole?"

"Yes, it is."

"But why?"

"Because…" said George. "It's just—I always thought that Marianne and I were soulmates, you know? Like, they say that each person has one true match out there. I really believe that. And I thought that Marianne and I were 'it' for each other."

"So you figured if you'd never been born, Marianne would remain single, grow old before her time, and become a dour spinster with bad glasses and her hair pulled too tight in a bun?"

"I don't know." George sank onto the edge of the bed and stared absently at the floor. "Something like that…Yeah."

"Is that not the most hideous window treatment you've ever seen?" said Marianne.

"That designer's the worst," said Dennis. "But the colour's sort of nice. Maybe we should use that shade of purple in Sophie's room?"

"Maybe."

George leaped up and grabbed Terrance by the lapels of his overcoat. "I have to get out of here. Now," he said, hyperventilating. "Please, Terrance, get me out of here. *I don't want to be unborn!*"

Terrance waved his hand, and in a flash he and George were standing at the edge of the river where they had first met. George paced the bank until his breathing slowed to normal. He watched fat snowflakes fall into the water and dissolve away, thousands of individual snowflakes descending, disappearing.

"Well," said Terrance. "Now that you exist again, do you feel better?"

George sighed. "I don't know," he said. "I feel confused. And depressed. I honestly thought I had made more of an impact, that my life *meant* something. Now everything seems so random and pointless."

"I'm sorry, George. I told you. So what do you want to do about it?"

George tried to reflect upon all the things that Terrance had shown him, but his thoughts kept skipping back to the toboganning hill, how the snow sparkled like crushed diamonds in the sunlight, and how keenly he remembered the feeling of riding his Snow Warrior down the slope—a short, but exhilarating descent.

"...wonderful," murmured George, his eyes closed.

"What's that?" said Terrance

"My life," said George, "maybe it wasn't so important, after all, maybe I didn't make such a big impact or anything, but I enjoyed it. For the most part. At least until the financial ruin. I mean, isn't that enough?"

"I don't know. What do you think? Is it enough to enjoy life in your little bubble while all around you the world goes to hell in a handbasket? Poverty, George. Disease. Corruption. War. Environmental degradation. You're having a nice barbecue in the yard while entire nations starve. You're driving your SUV to the mall while ecosystems perish and species vanish. You're laughing at sitcoms while AIDS makes millions of orphans. You're relaxing with a good book in front of the fire while vast populations are being deracinated or butchered. Atrocities abound. Misery and injustice everywhere. Is it enough for you to enjoy your life? You tell me."

George stared out over the dark river. He was silent for a while, then his eyes brightened "Maybe," he said, "maybe I could try much harder to have a positive effect and make a difference? Like this woman I read about in the paper last week, an Australian who runs a free clinic in Ethiopia, for young girls who have fistulas—holes in their bladders from giving birth when their pelvises are too underdevelop—"

"Yes, yes," Terrance interrupted, "I'm familiar with the condition and the woman."

"Maybe I could do something like that!"

"Hmm," said Terrance.

"Or maybe I could join the David Suzuki Foundation, and spearhead a local campaign to fight global warming."

Terrance chuckled. "This from a man who won't even recycle his tuna-fish cans."

"They stink up the bins," said George defensively.

Terrance didn't say anything, he just shrugged. And slowly the light in George's eyes dimmed as he realized that he would never run a free clinic in Africa or devote his time to combatting the greenhouse effect.

He would never do anything like that.

"Well, George, the way I see it, you can either jump back into that water or return to your family and resume your ultimately insignificant life. What's it going to be?"

George walked away from Terrance to the edge of the river. He thought about going home. It was possible that by now Marianne's fury had died down somewhat. Maybe worry had taken the place of rage, and she'd be waiting up for him when he got home. Maybe, since it was Christmas Eve, the kids would be keeping a tender vigil as well. He would be greeted with shouts of relief and joy—*Daddy! Daddy!*—as he came through the door, his arms open, soon to be filled with family. And maybe Marianne would have spread the word to his friends and customers, and they'd be coming by with words of support, and maybe not just words. Oh it almost made him cry to think of it. Unlikely though, that the townspeople would rally so quickly on the eve of a major holiday. Probably it would just be Marianne waiting up, and the kids already in bed. Or maybe he would go home and find the doors locked like the last time he stormed out after an argument. Maybe he would have to crawl through the basement window, where, if he were lucky, he would find one of those itchy wool blankets dumped on the futon couch. Maybe Marianne would be locked in the bedroom, fouling up the place with the cigarettes she smoked, one after another when she was angry. And maybe the repo men had already been by to take back the plasma-screen TV he had bought her for Christmas, and she would start screaming at him again about the money he'd been giving to his mother every month, or call him a selfish prick for disappearing on Christmas Eve and making the kids worry. There was really to no way to know.

George stared up at the lighted bridge that led to his wife and children. He stared down at the swirling black water.

Terrance waited for George to make his decision. He inspected his fingernails. He whistled "Let Me Call You Sweetheart" and used a rock to scrape some mud off his Wellingtons. "Come on, George," he said, straightening up. "Make up your mind, and off you go." But when he turned to the edge of the riverbank, George was no longer there.

TRUTH

THEY WERE TO MEET at Starbucks at five o'clock. At five-thirteen, Leslie drained her small black decaf and checked her watch. Just then, Martin entered and scanned the faces in the café. He advanced toward her.

"Leslie?"

"Hi."

"Sorry I'm late. Have you been here long?"

"Yes," she said, "over twenty minutes. But I'm always a bit early."

"I'm usually late," he said, taking a seat. "I wonder if that's the first sign that we're not going to get along."

"I don't know," she said. "Do you want something, a coffee?"

He glanced at the menu above the counter. "I'm too cheap to pay more than a buck for a cup of coffee. Besides, I'm already buzzing. Just had two cups with another prospective partner at the doughnut shop around the corner."

"Oh." She frowned. "How did it go?"

"Not well. When we spoke on the phone, she neglected to mention the fact that she has kids. Three of them. Personally,

I don't care for children. Especially when there's more than one."

"I'm not wild about them either. My sister has two. They're always so filthy, you know?"

"I suppose, but that doesn't really bother me. What I object to is the way they divert all the attention to themselves. They're like little black holes, sucking up attention like light particles. You can't escape it. Even I fall for it. When I'm in a room with a kid, I find myself watching the kid, fake-chuckling at the kid's ostensibly cute antics, commenting on them...It's like when there's a TV on in a bar; you don't want to look at it, but it keeps sucking you back in. Doesn't matter what's on—infomercials, a curling match—it just sucks you right in, you know?"

"Hmm," she mused. "I think you might have psychological problems that are incompatible with my own."

He smiled and fished a package of gum from his jacket. He offered her a piece.

"Does my breath smell?" she asked.

"I can't tell from here. I was concerned about mine, actually." He popped one shiny white tablet and slid the pack toward her.

"I'm okay." She pushed it back across the table.

"So," he said, pocketing the gum, "you're fatter than I thought you would be. I mean, not repulsively so. I can deal with your type and level of fatness; it's just not what I expected. You look thinner in your photo."

"I'm pretty normal from the waist up. It's my legs and ass that are fat. I have a lot of cellulite on my ass."

"You should post a photo that includes your bottom half."

"I know, I've thought about that. But I'm afraid I'll scare people off. This way, I can meet someone in person and, you know, maybe there'll be chemistry there, maybe they'll find me so charming and intelligent that they won't mind the extra bit of weight."

"I guess that makes sense. You have a pretty face."

"Yes, I know. Thanks."

"But I don't find you particularly charming or intelligent."

"But we've only just met."

"That's true."

A woman in a pink sweatsuit sat down at a nearby table. She had a baby in a corduroy papoose strapped to her chest. Martin's eyes fixed on the gurgling infant.

"You actually look a lot better than you do in your photo," said Leslie, following his gaze. "And while it concerns me that such a good-looking man is single—presumably, you have some profound and fundamental character flaws—I am physically attracted to you, and am prepared to set aside my initial reservations."

The baby jammed a fist into its eye and began to yell. Leslie smiled sympathetically at its mother.

"Listen," said Martin, "do you want to get out of here? Grab a drink or something?"

IT WAS HOT OUTSIDE. The streets were crowded with Saturday people. Martin walked quickly and purposefully, passing several upscale watering holes.

"Look," said Leslie when they paused at a red light, "I wear high heels only when I don't have to stand for too long or walk anywhere. My feet hurt and I'd like to stop in there for a drink." She gestured to a hotel across the street.

"Hotel bars are notoriously expensive," said Martin. "There's a pub just a few blocks down from here. They serve cheap draft and it's close to my apartment. Even if we took a cab, it would be cheaper than going to that hotel. But I think we should walk it, since I don't know you well enough to share your pain or even care about your discomfort."

"You're pissing me off," said Leslie, "but I have a wedding to attend in three weeks and I'm afraid of what my so-called friends will think and say about me if I show up to another major event without a date."

The light turned green. They proceeded to the pub.

Leslie ordered a martini, dry, with olives. Martin ordered a draft beer.

"This isn't so bad, is it?" said Martin, dabbing the sweat from his forehead and settling back in his chair.

"The carpet smells like wet gerbils, the exposed midriff of the waitress makes me feel dumpy and inadequate, and this martini has far too much vermouth in it."

"It's a pub. You should order beer."

"Beer gives me gas. Also, I'm well on my way to becoming a bona fide alcoholic, and liquor, as they say, is quicker."

"You know, I've never been addicted to anything," said Martin. "Nothing, nada. And I find it difficult to sympathize with substance abusers—whether that substance is Häagen-Dazs or heroin. Having said that, I tend to be more forgiving of men who have problems with the bottle. In certain cases, I even view it as macho and stylish—a kind of Bukowski bravado, you know? But with women it strikes me as nothing more than intolerable weakness."

"I just had this image," said Leslie, "of taking the little plastic sword from my cocktail and plunging it into your larynx." She laughed and swallowed the last of her drink with a flourish.

"I have to say, the fact that you're a boozehound pretty much puts me off for anything long-term, but makes me wonder if I'll be able to take you home tonight and have insincere sex with you once you're sloppy drunk."

"It's entirely possible," said Leslie. Martin waved down the waitress and ordered another half-pint. Leslie ordered a double gin on the rocks with a twist.

"Thanks a lot, Jan," said Martin when the waitress brought their order. She faux-smiled and moved off. They sipped their drinks.

"So," said Martin.

"So," said Leslie.

"You're a talent agent."

"Yes," she said. "It's not very interesting and I don't particularly enjoy it. And if you're bringing this up because you happen to be a closet actor, or know someone who's trying to break into the business, I'm going to guzzle this as fast as I can and then bolt."

"I'm not and I don't."

"Good."

"I'm just trying to make conversation and discover, in a roundabout fashion, how successful you are and perhaps even how much money you earn."

"I earn quite a lot of money. How successful I am depends on how one defines success."

"Well, the money part is a good start. Do you have any movie stars on your roster?"

"No."

"TV?"

"No. Not unless you count commercials. Almost all of my commissions come from commercials and voice-overs. You know Microbe Man?"

"Of course. The germ-fighting superhero."

"I rep him, for example."

"Not terribly glam."

"No."

"You mentioned that your younger sister is in the biz?"

"She's a development exec at CBS. Very powerful and important. I'm quite proud of her but also intensely jealous. I would like her to fail."

"She has kids, right?"

Leslie nodded. "And a wonderfully supportive husband whom I happen to be hot for, and a gorgeous apartment, and a palatial summer home. Oh yes, and a golden retriever, which I find kind of cliché."

"Already I'm more intrigued by your sis than I am by you," said Martin. "And if she didn't have rug rats, I'd probably start dating you just to get to her."

"She's in remission from breast cancer," said Leslie. "When she told me she was ill—around seven years ago—the first thing I thought of was whether I was genetically predisposed. Then I had this flash of her husband and me seeking solace in each other's arms after her death.

"Very nice."

"Later, when I learned that she wouldn't have to lose her perfect left breast, I felt tremendous relief but also a tiny glimmer of indignation. I think I felt she would be easier to love without it." Leslie drained her drink and sighed. "Well, I guess I'll go home, put on *Blonde on Blonde*, turn out all the lights, and get shit-faced."

"Listen," said Martin, "my self-esteem will be temporarily boosted if I get you into bed tonight, and that waitress is making me horny. Why don't we go to my place? I have booze. It'll be cheaper than ordering another round."

Leslie mulled it over. "Why not. I have masochistic inclinations and I'm feeling self-destructive."

"Then it's settled," said Martin, signalling for the bill.

Leslie paid the tab, and they left.

MARTIN LIVED IN a recently constructed, loft-style condominium unit—large windows, hardwood veneer floors, useless ductwork painted white and suspended from the high ceilings for an industrial/artsy effect. It was a roomy suite, sparsely decorated with severe, monochromatic furniture.

"I would like to know at once," said Martin, tossing his keys into an ashtray by the door and dimming, ever so slightly, the halogen track lighting, "if you're as impressed as I feel you should be by my carefully coordinated, evidently upscale living space?"

"Mildly impressed," she said, "but mostly confused by the fact that you're clearly a cheap-ass, yet you own what I'm certain is a pricey, albeit shoddily built, condo in a decent location."

"I don't own it," said Martin, "I rent it. I'm obsessed with status and the need to appear successful."

"That would explain the oversized Patek Philippe on your wrist."

"So you noticed?" Martin admired his own timepiece.

"Almost immediately," said Leslie.

"It's a fake," said Martin with a mirthless smile.

"So, in addition to being shallow, you're also a poser?"

"Somewhat of a poser," said Martin, "and a little shallow. But it's not as simple as that. I happen to be reacting to early childhood influences. I come from a large family—four brothers, three sisters. My parents were immigrants, dirt poor, and completely unsuccessful in their tenacious struggle to achieve even lower-middle-class respectability."

"Boo-hoo," said Leslie. "Cry me a river."

"And now my half-baked dot-com business venture is stillborn, I'm up to my sternum in credit card debt, I had to give up my BMW, which was leased anyway, and my prospects for rewarding employment are rapidly fading."

"So, too, is my interest in you."

"Well," said Martin, "I think the cold-hearted lush needs a drink." He moved toward the open-concept kitchen area. "Make yourself comfortable."

"I'm not sure that's possible," said Leslie, perching on the edge of a moulded plywood bench. She watched him pour a half-tumbler of straight booze from a giant plastic bottle of no-name gin.

"Panty remover," said Martin, dropping two ice cubes into the drink. He stirred it with his finger, not bothering to turn his back.

"That's revolting," said Leslie. "If it weren't for the anti-bacterial properties of straight alcohol, I wouldn't dream of letting that pass my lips."

"You germ-phobic types really give me a pain," he said, handing her the glass.

"Aren't you having anything?"

"I wouldn't mind a beer, but I'm afraid I won't be able to get it up if I drink any more. Now then," he said, "would some music help to put you at ease and hasten our transition to the bedroom?"

"If it's the right music, probably."

"Why don't you pick something then?" He gestured to several CD towers beside the stereo. "I'm going to go take a piss and try to mask my chronic halitosis with a surreptitious tooth-brushing and repeated gargles of Listerine."

Leslie studied the titles on the racks. She was still looking them over when Martin returned from the bathroom.

"Do you like jazz?" he asked.

"I feel I should, but I don't."

"You're taking an inordinate amount of time to select something. Are you judging me by my discs?"

"Yes, I am," she said. "Most of your collection seems worthy but pretentious. You have all the important jazz—"

"Which I rarely listen to."

"And all the correct classical—"

"Which I never play."

"But your pop collection is varied and interesting and bears a lot of overlap with my own. And, most encouraging, you have more soul than I expected."

"How about this?" said Martin, pulling out *Sensuous Seventies Soul Grooves, Volume 3*.

"I love that series," said Leslie, "but isn't it a bit heavy-handed for a middle-aged white guy in Sperry Top-Siders to be playing such blatantly sexual African-American music on a first encounter such as this?"

"Perhaps. But since there's nary a James Brown tune on this particular compilation, I believe it's within bounds."

Moments later, Leslie was undulating, drink in hand, to the mellifluous sounds of Al Wilson singing "Show & Tell."

Martin watched her sip and sway, sway and sip with her eyes half-closed. "Aren't you drunk yet?" he asked.

"I'm just perfectly and beautifully tipsy," said Leslie. "And, provided you don't have herpes or any other disease that could be transmitted orally, I wouldn't mind at all if you kissed me now."

Martin took the glass from her hand and placed it on a speaker. Then he leaned in, found her lips, and kissed her lightly a couple of times. She drew him close and pushed her tongue deep into his mouth. After a few seconds, he pulled away slightly.

"I'm worried about my breath," he said.

"It ain't great," said Leslie. "And while it's a factor that would disturb me over time, I'm too turned on at the moment to give a rat's ass."

They smiled at each other and resumed smooching. Martin squeezed Leslie's left breast. "Sufficiently firm," he mumbled, "but difficult to tell with the bra on."

She moved her hand over his crotch, locating the hard-on. "I'm relieved to find that I'm making you horny," she said and reached for the zipper in his pants.

"Let's go to the bedroom," he whispered.

"Wouldn't it be more spontaneous, more like an exciting Hollywood movie starring Glenn Close, if you took me right here on the floor?"

"Yes. But it would be infinitely more comfortable to take you in the bed."

"And the condoms are in there," she said, allowing herself to be led, by hand, into the bedroom. "Nice sheet set, Martin."

"Thanks."

She ran her hand over the duvet cover. "Did a woman friend pick this out?"

"No, I did."

"You're not gay, are you?"

"I don't think so. I mean, I've never done it with a man. But occasionally when I'm masturbating or even having sex with a woman, I'll get this image of a good-looking guy stroking his large, naked penis."

"I can live with that," she said. "Um, before we get down to it, I should probably hit the bathroom. I'm prone to painful bladder infections, and my doctor told me I should urinate before and after sex."

"In there," he said, pointing.

"Be right back."

Martin fished out some condoms and placed a couple on the bedside table for easy access. Then he quickly stripped off his clothes and slid under the duvet. He did a breath check and sniffed his pits. He waited. He waited some more. He heard the water running. He heard the toilet flush. He heard the water again. Eventually, Leslie reappeared.

"What took you so long?"

"I was snooping through your medicine chest. Then I checked my nipples to make sure there were no unsightly hairs sprouting around them. After that, I emptied my bladder, and passed gas while the toilet was flushing so you wouldn't hear me. Finally, I gave my vagina a little freshening sponge bath with some wet toilet paper. I dried myself on your hand towel."

"Strip," he said.

She took off her shoes and started unbuttoning her blouse. "I would feel more comfortable if you turned out the light."

"But I want to see what I'm getting."

"I'm too ashamed of my body to undress in these harshly lit conditions."

Martin switched off the bedside lamp. A bit of streetlight spilled in through the window, barely illuminating Leslie as she shed her clothes and slipped into bed.

"My eyes haven't adjusted to the light yet," said Martin, "but from what I could tell, you look pretty good."

"That's a relief."

"Now, I just have to worry about a) whether you'll deem my penis to be of sufficient length and girth, b) maintaining an erection while I struggle into a condom, c) premature ejaculation, and d) performing sensually and acrobatically enough for you to be pleasured to the point of orgasm thereby concluding that I'm good in bed."

"I hope you're circumcised," she said, ducking under the duvet. "Any STDs I should be aware of?" came muffled from beneath the covers.

"Scabies in college, but I've been clean and tested since then," said Martin. And she took him into her mouth. He flipped back the cover to watch her. After several heated moments he said, "Stop, or I'll shoot."

"Yes, officer," she said slyly, "whatever you say."

"Stop that too. I'm not into silly role-playing." He pulled her toward him, then pushed her onto her back. He kissed her mouth and her neck. He massaged and licked her breasts. She held his head in her hands. She made no sound. "Are you enjoying this?" he asked.

"Very much, but I'm preoccupied with how they look."

"They're a bit lopsided and not as big as I'd like, but they're reasonably firm and attractive."

She smiled and relaxed her grip on his skull. He kissed slowly down her belly, pausing just below the navel.

"Keep going," she said.

"I don't really want to. I don't like doing that. But I will, just to demonstrate that I'm a conscientious lover." He continued moving down.

"Mmm," she said. "You're not very skilled, but it feels good nonetheless."

"Enjoy it while you can. I only do it on first encounters." After about fifteen seconds, Martin sat up, reached for a condom, and tore open the packet. He rolled onto his back and slid it on. "Listen," he said, "I'm kind of pooped from my spinning class this morning—why don't you climb aboard?

"Because I'm submissive, and I prefer to be on my back or my knees."

"Oh, all right." He got on top.

"Ow," she said, "you're on my hair."

"Sorry." He adjusted his position. "How's that?"

"That's nice. Mmm, that's *very* nice."

Slowly they got into the rhythm of the thing. Leslie closed her eyes. She began to moan, softly at first, then not so softly.

"What are you thinking about?" he whispered.

"Brad Pitt," said Leslie.

"Me too," said Martin. And before long, with a grind and a whimper from Leslie, and a clenched-jaw growl from Martin, it was all over. He collapsed onto her, then rolled off with a sigh. He removed the condom carefully, tying it closed with a knot and examining it for defects. He placed it on the bedside table, crossed his hands over his belly, and closed his eyes. Leslie wiped the sweat from her face and pulled the duvet up over her body. *Sensuous Seventies Soul Grooves* came to what seemed an abrupt end, and all they could hear was faraway traffic and the sound of their own breathing.

"How do you feel?" asked Martin, his eyes still shut.

"Dejected," said Leslie.

"You came though?"

"I faked it."

"Oh." He turned onto his side, his back to her.

"Are you angry?"

"No. I'm disappointed. Ashamed. I can't seem to do anything right these days."

"I'm sorry," said Leslie, "I just wanted it to be satisfying for you, so that you might want to see me again and repeat the experience."

"Why the hell would *you* want to?"

"Because it felt warm and good, because I crave physical human contact, because it's been more than a year since I've had sex, because I'm tired of going for massages just to have another person's hands on my body." She exhaled and stared at Martin's broad back.

"I feel afraid," he said quietly.

"Of what?"

"Failure. Poverty. Ridicule. Death."

"Yes," she said. "And disease. Loneliness. Aging."

The mournful howl of a distant siren dopplered through the air.

They reached for each other in the dark room.

LOST KITTEN

SHE HADN'T LOST a kitten, but she called the number anyway. Two rings before a man picked up. "Hello?" Music played in the background. "Hotel California."

"Hi," she said. "I'm calling about the kitten?"

"Oh wow, great. Hold on a sec…"

The music faded. A sound like a dish clinking in a sink, then a cigarette being lit close to the phone.

"Yeah, hi," said the man. "Sorry about that."

"No problem."

"So, I guess I have your kitten, eh?"

"Um, I hope so."

"Well, I'd be surprised if there were more than one kitten missing in this complex, but just for laughs, can you describe her?"

She studied the poster taken from the lobby of her building. A crude line drawing of a cat face; no indication of colouring. These things usually included a photocopied snapshot. "Well, she's very tiny and very sweet."

The man laughed. "Most kittens are."

"And she's, um, kind of a mix of colours."

"Like calico?"

"Yeah, exactly. Calico."

"I guess this is her," said the man.

They made arrangements for her to collect the kitten that evening at seven. She plucked her eyebrows and gave her hair a v-05 Hot Oil treatment. He went to the mall to purchase a calico kitten.

THE COMPLEX IN WHICH she and the man lived contained five, twelve-storey high-rises positioned at various angles around a large and elaborate series of fountains. It was constructed in the 1950s, and it had a breezy, space-age look to it, one that exuded planning and optimism. The fountains now were dry and crumbling, but she remembered when they flowed. When she was a little girl in the 1960s, her mother would bring her to see the swans that lived in the fountains from June until September. Her mother said the swans were a secret that only they and the residents of the surrounding apartments knew about. Other people had to go to the Riverdale Zoo or Centre Island if they wanted to see swans, but they knew about these secret, private ones, and could visit whenever they liked without having to pay admission or contend with crowds. Whenever her mother felt a mood indigo coming on, they would get in the put-put—the rusting, 1958 Renault that Morris had given them—and drive to Moishe's on Bathurst Street. They would get two buttered bagels, one plain bagel, and a double-double coffee to go. They would head downtown to the fountains, where they would eat their buttered bagels and feed the plain one to the swans. The buttered bagels were wrapped neatly in wax paper. Her mother would give her sips from the coffee, and always saved the last and most sugary sip for her to dip her bagel into. It would soak up the sweetness and turn brown and wonderfully soggy. They would watch the swans in the space-age fountains, and they would feel good.

"Someday, we'll get an apartment here," her mother would say, "with a balcony that overlooks the fountain, and a bedroom for each of us." She'd say, "All it takes is dough, kiddo." She'd say it again on their way out of the complex, as they admired the cars in the parking lot. Big Pontiacs, Oldsmobiles, Fords, and Chryslers that were rust-free and didn't have cigarette burns or splits in the seats with foam sticking out. Sometimes they'd play they were shopping for a new car. She would pick the red Thunderbird with the black interior. Her mother would take the Cadillac convertible, if it happened to be in the visitor parking that day. Once, they got right into the white Cadillac and pretended to drive it. Her mother was unafraid, even lit her Craven A with the car's cigarette lighter. "All it takes is dough, kiddo," she said, blowing smoke, and adjusting her sunglasses in the rear-view mirror.

They never did get an apartment there. Not together. She moved in soon after Morris had his heart attack, about a year after her mother died, nearly five years ago. She didn't want to move out of the apartment she had shared with her mother for as long as she could remember, but the two men said she had to leave. They came to the door and said they were Morris's sons, and that they owned the building now that he was dead. They called her Geraldine—her mother's name—and wanted to know why she hadn't paid a cent of rent for the past forty years. She told them she wasn't her mother, and that she didn't know why they hadn't paid rent, but guessed it was probably because they were friends with Morris.

"Friends, eh?" said the skinny one. "What kind of friends?"

"Good friends," she said. "He gave us cars."

"He gave you cars?" The fat one looked at his brother.

"I knew it," said the skinny one.

"And he'd come see us once a week. And bring Turtles, or kielbasa, sometimes Tia Maria."

"What kind of cars?" said the skinny one.

"Well, first there was the put-put. That was a Renault. Then there was a Cutlass Supreme—we liked that one 'cause it was big, and it lasted a long time. Then there was the Pontiac. And after that was the—"

"Honda Accord, right?

"Right."

"And then, let me take a wild guess: a Toyota Camry?"

"How did you know?"

The brothers looked at each other and laughed

"Unbelievable," said the fat one.

"A trade-in of sorts," said the skinny one.

She didn't understand the joke, but she laughed to be polite. "The Toyota was the last one," she said. "It's still in the parking lot. I don't know how to drive, but I like to go sit in it. I like to listen to the radio. Sometimes I pretend to drive."

Again the brothers exchanged a look.

"Maybe we should talk to your mother," said the fat one. "Is your mother here?"

"No," she said, instantly having to fight back tears. "My mother is in heaven now."

They were nice to her after that. The fat one told her that everything was going to be OK and to stop crying and not worry about the rent she owed. He said they'd figure something out. The skinny one asked if she happened to have a picture of her mother. She couldn't help laughing at that. She had thousands of pictures of her mother. That was one of their favourite things to do, take Polaroids of each other. She invited the brothers in for a cup of Taster's Choice, and to look at photos—not any naked ones, of course, those were private—just the ones that were on display on the walls, shelves, windowsills, and fridge. The brothers seemed impressed by the images. They kept saying wow, and calling each other over to look at this one or that one. They lingered long in front of the brass étagère, checking out the series in which she had done her mother as different nationalities—in a beret and trench coat for French, fur hat and muff for Russian, bathrobe with a bolster pillow fastened with a sash around the waist for Japanese, a towel turban and lots of beaded necklaces for Ethiopian. Her mother would make the costumes and set up the shots. She would take the pictures.

"This is really something," said the fat one.

"Yeah," said the skinny one. "I think I see a lot of therapy in my future."

She offered them another cup of Taster's Choice, but they said they had to go.

"You mind if I take one of these?" The skinny one pointed to a group of photos of her mother, wearing cut-off shorts and a bathing suit top. She was stretched out on the hood of the Cutlass Supreme, reclining on the windshield with a Craven A burning in her hand. Her nails were long and red. Her blonde hair was done up in pigtails.

"What the hell for?" said the fat one.

"Just to have. It's Dad's history, after all."

"I don't think that's such a good idea," said the fat one.

"Why not?"

"'Cause certain people can never find out about Dad's little history."

"How would she find out?" The skinny one raised his voice. "Even if she found this—which she won't, I mean, how the hell would she?—she wouldn't know who it was or what the hell it meant."

"She'd recognize the car."

"Oh that's rich. Half the time she doesn't even recognize us."

"Yeah, but it's the old stuff she remembers."

"But she's not going to see it!"

"Uch," said the fat one. "Why don't you just leave it alone?"

"Are you sure you don't want another Taster's Choice?"

"No!" they said in unison.

She hated when people raised their voices.

"So, can I borrow this?" said the skinny one, softening his tone.

"I guess…" Even though she had half a dozen variations of the same shot, she didn't want to part with it.

"Actually," said the fat one, "do you mind if I quickly use your bathroom before we go?"

She said she didn't mind, but in truth she wanted them out already. Except for their brown hair and green eyes, they were nothing like Morris. Morris never raised his voice. He was always gentle and nice.

After the brothers left, she went into the bathroom to make sure the fat one hadn't stolen any of the Polaroids in there. He hadn't. But he had cleaned out her brush. She looked for the rectangle of hair in the wastebasket, but found nothing except used tissues and sanitary pads. He must have flushed it down the toilet. Why would he do that? Was he trying to send a message that she wasn't tidy enough, that she should empty her brush more often? That was no way for a guest to behave. And she had just been thinking that the fat one wasn't as bad as the skinny one, and that she could probably get used to him being the new Morris. She hoped she had seen the last of the brothers. Unfortunately, a couple of weeks later they returned. That's when they told her she owed more than $200,000 in back rent, not including interest payments. She said it sounded like a lot, and that she would have to phone her friend, Mr. Pantalone, at the bank. But the brothers said no, that she didn't have to call Mr. Pantalone, that they were prepared to forget about the debt if she signed some papers and moved out by the end of the following month. They told her they would help make the necessary arrangements.

There was only one place she could think of to go.

She stepped out onto the balcony and stared across the crumbling fountains to the other high-rises in the complex, wondering in which the man with the kitten resided.

HE HOPED SHE WOULD be almost pretty, but not pretty. Pretty wouldn't have anything to do with him, but he might have a chance with almost pretty. Brunette would be good. And young. The younger the better, he thought, as he piled dirty plates inside the oven and used a stiff dish towel to flick macaroni remnants off the counter into the sink. His roommate, Glen, had refused to clean up his dinner mess, and now he was stuck with the task if he wanted the place to look halfway presentable. It was ten minutes to seven. He didn't have time to do a proper tidying.

"Why don't you get her to clean up if it's so freakin' important?" Glen said. He didn't understand the concept of guests, particularly female ones, and seemed, in fact, to resent them. "We *need* a woman to clean up after us." Glen pounded his fist on the counter. "And to make us steaks."

"Look, why don't you just disappear for a while? Go to your room or something."

"No way, José. I want to check out this kitten chick, see if she turns out to be some kind of slut or feminazi."

"And what if she's a sweet little old lady? Huh? What if she's a nice innocent girl?"

"If she's a sweet little old lady, you're not going to invite her in. Are you, pal?"

He didn't answer.

"You're going to jam kitty through the door and call it a night. But, hey, if she happens to be a nice, innocent girl— a young one like you like—I'll leave you alone, buddy. I'll go crash for a while. Hell, you know that. But first I gotta see what shows up at our door, okay? 'Cause if it's one of those braless man-eaters with her lesbo tits hanging out, or her legs all hairy and gross, I might have something to say to the gal."

"Oh really, like what?"

"Um...like: your ugly-ass unshaven legs aren't gonna make you equal to me, and aren't proving anything except that you're a stupid cow who needs to become acquainted with a razor."

He sighed. Sometimes he really didn't like his roommate. Sometimes he just wanted to be rid of him. Glen was his oldest friend though. His only friend now. They'd been practically inseperable since they were kids. He couldn't just ditch the guy, but he often wished Glen would shut the hell up.

"Oh, for Christ's sake, shut that cat up, why don't ya," Glen said.

The kitten had been meowing for a while, so he scooped it out of its cardboard carton and cuddled it under his chin. He'd held kittens before, but never one as tiny as this. He brushed its fur against his lips and inhaled the warm kitteny fragrance. It reminded him of something, and made him feel sad, but before he could place what it was or why, Glen laughed and said:

"Hey, remember when your Dad *plonk*..." He mimed dropping something into a plastic grocery bag. "And then *wham* on the side of the house."

"Oh leave me alone, for Christ sake!" There was knock at the door then, and he knew for certain that his outburst had been heard in the hall. "Thanks a lot, Glen," he hissed as he leaned down to check his reflection in the kettle.

"Such a handsome devil," Glen said with a fakey gay accent. Then he blew a big kiss to his friend's reflection.

It was exactly 7:00 p.m.

THROUGH THE PEEPHOLE he discerned the following: old— late thirties, or even older—but pretty. A brunette, like he liked. And something soft about her. Something meek in the posture. He opened the door wide.

"Hi," he said. "Sorry about that. My roommate is being a jerk."

"Oh," she said. "It's OK, um…"

"Kitten," said the man, stepping back and aside. "Come on in. I'll just get her for you."

She hesitated on the threshold, peeking into the apartment, which looked both familiar and strange. It had the same layout as her own, and the same parquet flooring, which is how she knew it was the same size (three squares by four squares for the vestibule) even though it looked much smaller. The man had a couch and a chair and a TV in the same spots where she had a couch and a chair and a TV, but his were twice the size of hers and took up a lot more space. Also, the man had covered the large picture window and the window on the balcony door with green garbage bags and duct tape instead of blinds or curtains. The total lack of view made the suite seem shorter. Stubbier.

"It's okay," he said, smiling, gesturing for her to enter. "Glen's gone to his room."

The apartment smelled like cigarette smoke, which she liked. She stepped inside and closed the door behind her as the man disappeared into the kitchen.

She had seen flags over windows before but never garbage bags. The only indication that it wasn't totally dark
outside were tiny cracks of light peeking through here and
there where a bag sagged or the silver tape had peeled back a
smidgeon. She noticed the faint sound of TV coming from
behind a closed door down the hall. Laugh track. And the
exaggerated voices of sitcom characters.

"Here she is," said the man, returning with the kitten.

"Oh," she said. "So cute!"

As he handed it over, he noticed that the woman wasn't
wearing a wedding or engagement ring, or any jewellery for
that matter. She had nail polish on, but it was a soft pink,
practically transparent. Nothing garish about that. Even
Glen, who despised nail polish, couldn't call it trampy. Her
nails weren't too long either. She seemed clean and well-
groomed.

"Sweetie-pie…" said the woman, nuzzling the kitten.
"Hello, sweetie pie."

"Is that her name? Sweetie-pie?"

"Her name? Oh, no. It's not Sweetie-pie. It's, um, Geraldine."

"Geraldine." The man laughed. "That's a funny name for a
cat."

"I guess," said the woman, blushing and looking away.

He liked that she blushed and looked away. It made her
seem young even though she was old, at least ten years older
than him, at least thirty-eight, maybe more. He had the urge to
erase some of those years by switching off the overhead light,
but decided not to even dim it just yet. No point in scaring her

off. "Listen," he said. "I was just about to give kitty—I mean, *Geraldine,* a dish of milk. Would you like to come in for a minute? Maybe have a cold beverage?"

"Oh," she said. "Okay."

"Don't worry about Glen. He's not going to bother us, I don't think. Have a seat," said the man. "What would you like to drink?"

"Um, do you have any Tia Maria?"

"Oh, jeez. I don't think so." *Tia Maria?* "Um, I have some airplane bottles of Bailey's in my room. You know, I might even have a Kahlua," said the man. "That's pretty much the same, isn't it?"

"I don't know."

"Want me to check?"

"OK."

"Be right back."

Of course, he wasn't even halfway down the hall before Glen was on his case about the girl and her drink of choice.

"Tia Maria?" Glen whispered. *"Tia fuckin' Maria?"*

"So what?"

"So it looks like the lady is a lush, my friend. Too bad, 'cause she doesn't look too skanky on the surface, does she?"

He ignored Glen and slipped into his room.

"Come on, guy, think about it. What kind of woman waltzes into a strange man's apartment, then demands booze even though she was just offered a cold beverage, which, in my book, clearly means a glass of pop or juice?"

"Tia Maria is a girlie drink," he said, balancing on a chair to retrieve the miniature bottles of liqueur from atop the bookshelf. "I don't think you can conclude she's a lush 'cause she asked for an ounce of Tia Maria. She probably just has a sweet tooth."

"Speaking of which, that tooth, sweet or not, is kind of long, don't you think?"

"She looks alright to me." He used a T-shirt from the laundry basket to wipe the thick pad of dust off the bottles. "These are still fine, don't you think?"

"Sure. Bottoms up. If the lush gets ptomaine poisoning, it's her own damn fault."

"We don't know that she's a lush, okay? So butt out. Piss off."

"Yeah, yeah. We'll see how things go. If she gets drunk and starts whoring it up, I'm coming out."

"Don't start, okay? Please." He pressed a hand to his left temple and sighed deeply. "And can you turn off that TV?"

"Sure, *Sigh* Sperling, Mr. *Sigh* Master. Better run along. You know how nosy these girls can get. Don't want her poking through your things while your gone. Don't want her straightening the sofa pillows, now do you?"

SHE TOUCHED THE kitten's nose to her own. "Don't worry," she whispered. "You're going to come live with me. It'll be fun." She hoped that whoever had really lost the kitten wouldn't be too sad about it. She wondered why it hadn't occurred to her to get a pet before now.

"Here we go," said the man, entering with a drink in one hand and a saucer of milk in the other. "Hey, what happened to your shirt?"

She glanced at her tank top.

"You took your shirt off."

"I took my cardigan off," she said. "It's really warm in here."

The man sighed and set the saucer of milk down on the floor. Glen was going to have a field day with this development. Now she was not just a lush, she was also a tramp. At least she was wearing a bra, he noted, as he handed her her drink. Thank god for that.

"Thank you very much." She set the kitten down in front of the saucer and watched it tongue up the milk. Little flicks of pink. So sweet.

The man sat at the opposite end of the brown sofa. One large vinyl seat cushion separated them. The faux-leather was covered in strips of criss-crossing duct tape.

"You're not having one?" she said, swirling the ice in her glass.

"I'm not really thirsty. But I'll smoke, if you don't mind."

"I don't mind."

He lit a cigarette, then offered her the pack.

"No, thanks." She took a sip of her drink. "Mmm. What did you say this was?"

"Bailey's Irish Cream."

"Bailey's Irish Cream?"

"Yeah."

"It's good."

"Glad you like it." With dismay, he watched her drain the rest of the drink. Now he would have to offer her another, with Glen, no doubt, listening in the hallway. Great. At least she didn't smoke. Glen disapproved of women who smoked. He thought it was unladylike. He said it wrecked their eggs and made their babies feeble. If she smoked, Glen would probably be out here already, stirring up the shit, making his life difficult.

She set her glass on the upside-down milk carton that served as a side table. She licked her lips.

"Would you like another?" he asked, telepathically willing her to decline.

"Yes, please."

"How about some food with that? I've got Bits 'n' Bites. Or some Bugles?"

"No, thank you. Just Bailey's Irish Cream, please."

As he poured out another mini-bottle, he noticed that the largest butcher knife, the one they called "Ralph," was missing from the block. He checked the cutlery drawer. No go. Earlier, he had transferred the dirty dishes from the sink into the oven, so he knew it wasn't in there. From the kitchen doorway he looked down the hall. Sure enough, there was Glen, squatting on his heals, rocking and smirking, smirking and rocking, with his hands behind his back. Time for some damage control. He returned quickly to the living room.

"Here you go. Cheers."

"Thank you. Mmm, yum."

"It's funny," he said, lighting another cigarette. "You don't strike me as a drinker."

She laughed. "I'm not a drinker. I mean, ever since Morris died, I don't drink at all. Except for now."

"You see, I knew you weren't a drinker."

"How did you know?"

"Well...your complexion, the way you're dressed. I'm really glad you're not a drinker."

"Thanks."

"So who's this Morris?"

"My mom's friend."

"Oh."

"And my friend. He used to bring us Tia Maria."

"Oh yeah."

"He died about four years ago."

"That's too bad."

"Yeah. He brought Tia Maria even after my mom died."

"That was nice of him—hey, are you OK?"

"Yeah. I just...I really miss my mom." She wiped tears from her eyes and turned her face away from the man. That's when he noticed Glen, sneaking a peek at the woman, or more specifically, at her breasts, which were not too large, but had depressingly prominent nipples pressing against an insufficiently padded bra and tank top.

No words for half a minute, just the sound of the woman sniffling, and the man smoking. Then he coughed and said, "What's this?" He rubbed his thumb and index finger together.

"I don't know."

"The world's smallest violin." He laughed.

She laughed too. She thought it was nice of him to try to cheer her up with a funny joke. "Morris had brown hair and green eyes like you," she said.

"Is that right?"

"Yeah." She picked up the kitten, which had finished the milk and had started to meow. "Anyway...I guess I could go and buy my own Tia Maria. I just never think of it, you know."

"Well, that's good."

"It is?"

"Yeah...I mean, drinking can be very bad for your health." The man laughed loud and long.

She didn't get the joke, but smiled anyway. This man had a good sense of humour. In the magazines she read, women were always saying that was the most important thing. They were always looking for a man with a good sense of humour. And now she had found one. The weird thing was she had seen this man before, walking down the street toward the corner where the stores were, or walking back with grocery bags. He was one of the dozens of people she saw again and again, walking out of the complex toward the stores and the subway, or walking home from there. Sometimes if it was hot in her place, she would sit on the bench at the entrance of the complex and watch the people funnel in with their bags of food and disappear into their apartments. Later, she would stand on her balcony, staring out, and see those same people standing on their balconies, staring out. Five giant rectangles with people funnelling in and staring out. But now she had been invited into this man's apartment. A man she had passed on the street numerous times but never thought anything about. A man with a good sense of humour. The reality of this, plus the Bailey's Irish Cream and the kitten nuzzling soft against her ankle, made her feel happier than she'd felt in years.

"I've seen you before," she said.

"Oh really?" The man, still laughing a little, wiped tears from his eyes.

"Walking down Lawton."

"I guess that makes sense. How long have you lived here?"

"Almost four years."

"Hmm. And what is it that you do?"

"Um. I go to the movies, or stay home and watch TV, or I go to restaurants or the park…"

"No, I mean what do you for a living? Where do you work?"

"Oh I don't work. Work is for suckers."

"Excuse me?"

"Work is for suckers. My mom used to say that."

"Is that right?"

"Yeah. She said life is too short to waste on work or worrying."

"So she never worked?"

"No."

"But your dad worked."

"I never had a dad."

"Never?"

"Never."

"Well, I guess some people have all the luck."

She shrugged.

"So your mom never worked, and you've never worked."

"That's right."

"Must be nice."

"Yeah, it's nice."

"Well, it's not like I'm a big fan of it or anything. I mean, my job totally bites, actually. But what if everybody felt that way? What if everyone thought work was for suckers?"

"I don't know…"

"What if the garbage man didn't pick up your garbage? Huh? What if the firemen were kicking back, having a beer, while your house burned to the ground? Hm? What if there was no doctor to sew your ear back on if a dog bit it off?"

"That would be bad."

"Certainly it would bad. It would be worse than bad." The man stubbed out his cigarette, then lit another. He inhaled deeply and blew smoke through his nostrils. "What, are you rich or something?"

"I don't think so."

"You don't know?"

"Mr. Pantalone, at the bank, takes care of things."

"Where'd you grow up?"

"Bathurst and Wilson."

"Monster home?"

"Pardon?"

"Big house?"

"No. We lived in an apartment."

"Doesn't sound rich. So if your mom never worked, how did she pay the rent?"

"We didn't pay rent. Morris owned the building."

"Oh. I see. *Shit*." The man hunched forward and closed his eyes.

"What's wrong?"

"Nothing." He pressed the palm of his hand hard against his left temple.

"Are you okay?"

The man didn't answer. He sat hunched for a moment, then relaxed back on the couch and took a deep drag on his cigarette. "I think your mom worked," he said. "I think she worked for buddy who brought the Tia Maria. Maybe you worked for him too?"

"Morris was our friend." She set her empty glass down on the side table. She licked her lips.

"How about some more Bailey's Irish Cream?"

"Um, I don't know." She was already feeling warm and dizzy from the first two. It was awfully nice stuff though.

"Come on, one more won't kill you," the man said, heading for the kitchen. "Hey, you mind if I turn off the overhead light? My eyes are kind of sensitive to light."

"I don't mind. Can I use your bathroom?"

"End of the hall. Excuse the mess. My roommate is a slob."

AS HE POURED the last bottle of Bailey's into her glass, he could feel the dread rising from the solar plexus into his throat. "Please," he whispered. "Just go back to your room. You've got it all wrong."

"You think?" Glen smirked in the warped reflection of the kettle. "You figure Miss Guzzle-Liquor-in-a-Strange-Man's-Apartment is a virgin or something?"

"It's possible. I mean, she seems...I don't know. Don't you think there's something off about her?"

"Off? I'll tell you what's *off*. Her shirt, after about five minutes in a strange man's apartment. She's all: *doopsy-doo, check out the headlights, boys!* You think she's expecting to leave here without getting nailed? Huh? You think the slag's not expecting a cock up her hole?" Glen adjusted his penis, which was stiffening in his pants. "Why do you think she's getting so lubed? She's getting ready to take it up the ass."

When Glen got excited, he was difficult to control. "Just calm down, okay?"

"Oh I'm calm, don't you worry."

"Where's Ralph?" He gestured to the knife holder.

"You know damn well," Glen snapped.

"Put it back."

"I think I'll just keep it handy if it's all the same to you."

"It's not all the same! What if she's—?"

"What? *Sweet? Innocent?* I'll tell you what, pal, if you put the moves on her and she tries to stop you, I mean, *really* tries to stop you, then we'll call it a night, OK. We'll send her and her calico pussy back into the world. Hell, maybe you can call her up sometime. Take her to a Renée Zellweger movie. Bring her some Tia fuckin' Maria." Glen laughed loud but stopped abruptly. "Holy shit," he said. "You'd actually like that, wouldn't you?"

"Yes," said the man. "I would."

SHE FLUSHED THE TOILET, and washed her hands, drying them on her pant legs. She didn't want to touch the filthy towel hanging from a hook on the back of the door. The bathroom was a mess, and smelled awful—sharp, like ammonia. Why would the man live with such a dirty roommate? Maybe the man was dirty too. She wondered which one of them owned the toothbrush in the cup on the sink. It was caked with dried, yellowing toothpaste, and the bristles were all grey and bent back. It had to be at least five years old. Or maybe it looked that way because they both used it. There was only one toothbrush in the bathroom. Did roommates share toothbrushes? She hoped not. She wanted to kiss the man, but not if he shared a toothbrush with his roommate. Was that the kind of thing she could ask about if he started to kiss her? Probably he would think she was rude. She would just have to kiss him back that's all. A man with a good sense of humour was worth it. And then maybe, after the kissing and everything, he would visit her once a week, and get into bed with her, and bring her things. Maybe he would give her a car, and teach her how to drive it. She opened the medicine cabinet, but there was nothing there except toenail clippers and prescription pills. She checked behind the shower curtain. One bar of soap. One dirty razor.

She wondered, as she returned to the living room, if the man and his roommate shared more than just a toothbrush.

THE VIRTUAL TOUR

MARLA WAS EXHAUSTED. She hadn't slept properly since the relationship ended, which explains to a degree why she did what she did. Not long ago she was bagging nine hours of plum slumber a night, and that was on a stone-age futon, that was with a man who snored. The three of them had been together since college—Marla, Brian, and his so-called bed, a double futon *sans* frame. It was an evil thing that, like an old dog, smelled worse each year and grew strange lumps. They hated it. Her especially. They would get in, nestle into their respective Brian/Marla-shaped indentations, and talk about buying a new bed, a real bed with mattress and box spring, one of those fluffy football fields from Sleep Country Canada, one of those behemoths that are almost as tall as they are wide. But it was not to be. After buying a house in Toronto, even one billed as "condo alternative in Bloorcourt Village, needs TLC" (i.e., quark-sized dump in dodgy neighbourhood), purchasing a new bed was about as realistic as springing for a private jet. They didn't buy anything. They bought food. And mousetraps. And lottery tickets.

Brian wasn't as keen on homeownership as Marla was. She had house lust. She'd always had it. When she was a kid in the late 1960s, her parents took her driving downtown one Sunday. They wanted to show her how the poor people lived, and how lucky she was to reside in a shiny new subdivision just south of Steeles Avenue. They trolled slowly through Cabbagetown, pointing at the old men drinking beer and smoking cigarettes on their front stoops, pointing at the undershirts, pointing at the tattoos. But Marla didn't feel lucky; she felt envious. She loved the sagging porches and peeling paint and unruly dandelion lawns. These were houses like she had never seen in the suburbs—storybook houses with stained-glass windows and wooden pillars, steeply pitched roofs and gingerbread trim. Houses with gables and balconies, windowed dormers in the attic, and sometimes even turrets. She felt in her gut that she had always known them. A correspondence.

As soon as she was old enough, Marla moved downtown. The plan was for her to stay on the pullout couch in her aunt's (disappointingly new) condo in Village by the Grange, while she attended the Ontario College of Art. Marla slept at her aunt's place twice. On the third day of school, a classmate, the cute video artist named Brian, invited her to his Baldwin Street apartment for dinner—homemade yellow pea soup and a case of Molson Ex. She never left.

Marla and Brian were instantly simpatico, and remained remarkably in step given their different backgrounds and personalities. Brian was a fourth-generation Canadian from Weyburn, a small farming community in Saskatchewan. Marla was the daughter of Holocaust survivors who fled post-war Prague to seek refuge in the bosom of Bathurst Manor. Brian was calm, friendly, outdoorsy. Marla was nervous, misanthropic, agoraphobic. Brian was frugal; Marla, a spendthrift. Brian liked to hike the Bruce Trail on the weekend. Marla liked to troop through open houses. Somehow, they hit it off. They had the same taste in books, movies, music, and art. They both loved to sleep long, eat well, and dance drunk in the living room. Their sexual proclivities jibed perfectly. They shared a similar sense of humour, relished bad TV—Melrose Monday was a tradition throughout the 1990s—and had identical levels of mess tolerance (clutter was fine; dirt, unacceptable). They were together four years before they had their first argument. Brian agreed to babysit a friend's cat for the night; Marla was allergic to cats. They worked it out.

By the time Marla and Brian had saved enough cash to take out a high-ratio CMHC insured mortgage and leave the Baldwin Street love shack behind, they were almost thirty years old. Brian had been shooting corporate videos to support his art and supplement his income. Marla was exhibiting regularly, selling eight or nine canvases a year. They bought a hundred-year-old Victorian semi at Bloor and Lansdowne. They bought it at night, after seeing it once. The house turned out to need a lot more than "TLC," but as Marla told Brian while they sweated it out in the backseat of their agent's Audi during the curbside bidding war, the place had "good bones."

They went to work on it. Slowly, over the years, they nudged it into shape. They did everything themselves except for the wiring—a knob-and-tube conflagration in the making.

They ripped up broadloom and tore down ceiling tiles. They peeled linoleum and steamed wallpaper. They sanded, plastered, and plumbed. They stripped, varnished, and drywalled. One by one, they painted the rooms in rich, warm colours. Marla started an intricate mural on the walls of the master bedroom. They raked the car parts and crack pipes out of the yard. They put in tomatoes. And tulips. They furnished the house with stylish second-hand castoffs. Brian called the place "Value Village." It was filled with Goodwill.

Throughout the ongoing, ten-year renovation, they had only one big fight—a heated but short-lived shouting match involving hormones and a can of expensive paint that was aubergine in the store (when Marla bought it) but Popsicle purple on the dining-room walls (when Brian put it there while Marla slept in). It was: *You picked it!* and *How could you not realize it?!* It was: *Why didn't you wake me?!* and *This is the thanks I get!* Marla cried. Brian stormed out. He returned three hours later, drunk, with a slightly melted offering, a PMS-Buster Parfait from Dairy Queen. They ate ice cream and laughed and took Polaroids of the purple. Eventually, they primed, repainted, and continued to love and care for each other until Marla moved out so she could fuck somebody else.

His name was Alex. He was an artist who ran a gallery on Dufferin near Queen. He was talented, funny, and available. He was new. The first time she met him—at a friend's book launch—she thought about what it would be like to have sex with him. The second time they crossed paths, at a Vic Chesnutt concert at the Phoenix, he pulled her into the men's washroom and kissed her. It was shocking. Audacious. They started spending time together during the day while Brian was at work. Brian had given up on video art, and was doing corporate communications exclusively. Marla and Alex would meet in interesting places where they could kiss and grab— the Bat Cave at the museum, the Planetarium, the Henry Moore room in the AGO. It was romantic and playful, and as long as she kept her clothes on, it wasn't truly an affair. They would kiss and grab for as long as she could spare, then she'd rush home, clean up and prepare dinner. Now that Brian was working full-time, and paying a greater share of expenses, he expected the house to be tidy, and dinner on the go when he got in. It was only fair, but she started to resent it. What about *her* work? What about the days when she didn't see Alex, and toiled all day in her studio? Was she supposed to drop her brush at four-thirty and pick up the broom? On those days, Brian would come home and eyeball the cold stove and the dishes in the sink. He'd ask what's for dinner, and stare forlornly into the fridge. He would sigh and sigh. Marla started to feel like a housewife. She'd never thought of herself as housewife before. She didn't even want to be a *wife*, and had refused Brian's annual marriage proposals so she could remain the more youthful-sounding *girlfriend*.

The future began to scare. Was this it? Was Marla going to do what her mother had done (and regretted): hook up with her childhood sweetheart and stay with him until death did they part (in her mom's case, at age forty-seven with a tumour in the breast)? Would she never experience anyone new? She was thirty-nine years old and had only been with one man. An excellent man. A kind man. A man who was devoted to her, who would never leave her, and would undoubtedly stand by her if she got a tumour in her breast or became paralyzed in a car crash. A man with whom she shared almost a secret language, they'd been together for so long. A man who would never dream of kissing and grabbing someone else in the Bat Cave at the museum.

He was broken when she left. Even though she called it a Trial Separation. Perhaps somewhere in the back of her confused mind she thought she could taste freedom then return home when she was satiated and ready to resume her regular life.

Now, two years later, Marla lay awake in her cruddy apartment, in her two-thousand-dollar Sealy Posturepedic, desperately trying to get to sleep. Brian was married. Alex was grabbing somebody new. It was 3:47 a.m.

Marla got up and zombied to the computer. She had already tried TV and reading; perhaps surfing the Internet would do the trick. She checked her e-mail—there was none—then pulled down her favourites menu and clicked on *mls.ca*. The Toronto Real Estate Multiple Listing Service. Marla's porn. There were prices and photos and graphic descriptions. *Huge houses bare all*. Marla knew that unless she won a lottery, she would never again own a home in Toronto. But like an old lecher who could no longer get it up, she still liked to look and drool. Rosedale, Forest Hill, the Bridal Path. The more costly the house, the more likely it was to have a Virtual Tour, a nifty videotaped walkthrough of the property. You could select any room—master bedroom or solarium, for example—and then click on tiny arrows to pan around for a full 360° view.

Typically, Marla would start with the toniest areas and the most expensive listings, but sometimes for a laugh, she'd look at the cheapest homes in the city—the termite-infested shacks at Main and Gerrard, the Insulbrick abortions at St. Clair and Keele, the Seussian sinkholes on Shaw north of Bloor. And once in a blue moon she would check out the homes in her old neighbourhood, which is what she did on this night, which is how she found the photo that at first glance looked familiar, and upon closer inspection knocked the breath right out of her. It was her house, *not her house*, with a "for sale" sign on the front lawn. It was listed for $319,000 dollars. They had paid $165,000.

There was a virtual tour of the property.

With cold fingers, Marla clicked on "Living Room / Dining Room" and stared at the screen. The two rooms that used to be separated by plaster and French doors had been joined into one open-concept area. The (admittedly worn) hardwood floors had been covered in off-white broadloom, and the walls had been painted pastel peach. All the second-hand furniture had been replaced. The old pine dining table with its mismatched wooden chairs was now a glass and chrome thing with six identical straight-backed seats. The 1940s burgundy sofa was now a cream-coloured leather monstrosity, which, by the looks of it, would not have to have a cent paid for it until 2010. The crammed bookshelf was gone, as was the portrait Marla had done of Brian. A framed print, a vase of watercolour flowers, hung in its place.

Marla clicked "Kitchen" and saw that the walls were now pastel yellow, the painted plank floor had been tiled in hardware store linoleum, and the vintage cupboards had been swapped for white melamine. She clicked on "Hallway." The wooden stairs with their beautiful incurvatures, where a hundred years of feet had tread, had been carpeted. Worse, the intricate banister and railing that she'd spent months painstakingly stripping with heat gun and scraper—and was halfway through when she moved out—had been painted over in that same hideous pastel peach.

Marla felt nauseous. And betrayed. How could this happen? How could Brian have turned their home into a land of bland? Who was he really? And who the hell had he married? Marla had gathered the odd bit of information about the wife from Anthony, the only mutual friend who hadn't dropped her after the split. Her name was Tina; she was a thirty-three-year-old dental hygienist from Tweed, Ontario. Sweet and nice. Conservative. Outdoorsy. Apparently quite beautiful, but as Anthony assured Marla: "Zero sense of humour." "How did they meet?" she asked him. "The girl was vacuuming the saliva out of his mouth, honey. It was love at first suck."

After a trip to the kitchen for a shot of Canadian Club, Marla resumed her seat at the computer and clicked on "Bedroom." This second upstairs room had been her studio. Burnt orange walls. Canvasses everywhere. Now it was empty. White walls, white broadloom, not a trace of her remained. Marla steeled herself and clicked on "Master Bedroom." Her mural, the mural she had lovingly painted over a six-year period, the gorgeous trompe l'oeil garden paradise that grew organically from her brush and her soul had been wiped out with pastel peach. Incredulous, she stormed to the kitchen and swigged CC straight from the bottle. She stormed to the bathroom and stared at her face in the mirror. It was red with fury. Marla was far too riled to attempt sleep. She returned to the kitchen for another drink. She stood in fridge light, chomping angrily through a stalk of celery. Then she went back to the bathroom to take a leak. She didn't move when she was finished. She just sat there, hunched over with her Canadian Clubbed cranium resting on her bare thighs until she heard the thump of the weekend newspaper at her apartment door. She made coffee and got into bed with the classified section.

It was in there. "Sparkling Semi in Bloorcourt Village. Shows Beautifully!" There was an open house scheduled for later that day, between one and four. She thought about going to it. She thought about burning the place down. That's when she got the idea to do what she was going to do.

Yes.

Marla rifled through her supply cupboard until she found the old squeezy bottles of poster acrylic.

She chose blood red.

The house wouldn't show so beautifully when she was through with it.

MARLA ARRIVED AT 1:45 P.M. She didn't want to risk running into Brian or his bride on their way out (presumably, for some fabulous post-coital brunch). She stepped into the vestibule, into a cloud of vanilla perfume. A handwritten sign read: *Please remove shoes.* Marla hadn't thought of that. She had worn her sneakers for a quick getaway. Oh well. She would just grab them on her way out and run socked to the subway.

The agent, a brittle redhead in Banana Republic, was chatting with a young couple that had just come down the stairs. She smiled large at Marla. "Would you mind signing in," she said, gesturing to the pad of paper on the dining-room table.

Marla signed in as Frida Kahlo. She took a feature sheet and pretended to peruse it. "Well," she said, "maybe I'll start with the bedrooms."

When she got upstairs she peeked into the bathroom, which had not been included in the virtual tour. It had always been white, and looked pretty much the same except for a new shower curtain and bathmat, both pale peach. For some reason she opened the cupboard above the toilet and looked inside. An overjoyed blonde on the cover of a Nice 'n Easy box looked back at her. She slammed the thing shut and proceeded angrily to the master bedroom.

Marla closed the door behind her, and fished the paint out of her bag. Her heart was going like Buddy Rich on a mad snare. She glared at the pastel peach walls that had devoured her mural, and would now succumb to her red justice, but as she popped the lid on the squeezy bottle, she experienced a wave of dizziness and had to sit down for a moment. Marla noticed then how small the bed looked, and how hard it felt compared to her Sealy king-size. She pressed the heel of her hand into the mattress, and realized that it wasn't a mattress at all. It was a futon sunk into a bedlike frame. She flipped back the top of the duvet and peeled the peach-coloured fitted sheet off a corner. It was the stone-age futon from college. Their futon. Marla's nostrils filled with the familiar funky aroma. And there was another smell too, something comforting and scalpy coming off the pillow. It was Brian's smell. It was Brian.

Marla leaned in and inhaled. She pressed her face right into the pillow and breathed deeply into the lungs. A wave of warm flooded through her. *Two seconds,* she told herself as she stretched out and nestled into the Brian-shaped indentation.

Then, for the first time in more than two years, Marla fell instantly to sleep.

ACKNOWLEDGEMENTS

Thanks to my publisher, Lynn Henry, for cogent editing, and to Sarah MacLachlan and everyone at House of Anansi (I feel like I've found a home). Thanks to Kevin Connolly for paving the way there. Love and appreciation to the fine individuals who read my stories and provided valuable feedback: Randall Cole; Kevin Connolly; Gil Adamson; David Whitton; Terry Grogan; Stuart Ross. Thanks to Daphne Floros and Danny Rappaport for their help with medical information, and to Robyn Friedman and Alan Zunder for the goods on police procedure. Thanks to Ingrid Paulson for designing a nifty cover.

Danny/Robyn/Otto Friedman, thank you for support/babysitting/diapers. Thanks to Carol Kitai for keeping me alive and comparatively calm. Thanks to Randall Cole and Max Friedman-Cole for keeping me happy.

I am truly grateful to the Canada Council for the Arts, the Ontario Arts Council, and the Toronto Arts Council. Without their assistance over the years I wouldn't have been able to write what I wanted to write.

Earlier drafts of some of the work in this book appeared in the following publications: "The Soother" appeared previously in *Toronto Life*; "Truth" appeared previously in *The Malahat Review*, *The Journey Prize Stories*, and *03:Best Canadian Stories*; "Lost Kitten" and "Wonderful" appeared previously in *Taddle Creek*; and "The Virtual Tour" appeared previously in *The New Quarterly*.

MATTHEW PLEXMAN

ABOUT THE AUTHOR

Elyse Friedman has written two novels, *Then Again* (Random House Canada) and *Waking Beauty* (Crown US), and the poetry collection, *Know Your Monkey* (ECW). *Then Again* was a finalist for the 2000 Trillium Book Award, and the short story "The Soother" won the Gold National Magazine Award for Fiction in 2006. Friedman was born in Toronto, where she is currently raising her son, writing a new novel, and working on several screenplays.

Anansi offers complimentary reading guides that can be used with this work of fiction and others.

Ideal for people who love talking about books as much as they love reading them, each reading guide contains in-depth questions about the book that you can use to stimulate interesting discussion at your reading group gathering.

Visit www.anansi.ca to download guides for the following titles:

Long Story Short
Elyse Friedman
978-0-88784-803-2 • 0-88784-803-6

Day
A. L. Kennedy
978-0-88784-808-7 • 0-88784-808-7

Die With Me
Elena Forbes
978-0-88784-804-9 • 0-88784-804-4

The Outlander
Gil Adamson
978-0-88784-792-9 • 0-88784-792-7

The Tracey Fragments
Maureen Medved
978-0-88784-768-4 • 0-88784-768-4

Gargoyles
Bill Gaston
978-0-88784-776-9 • 0-88784-776-5

The Law of Dreams
Peter Behrens
978-0-88784-774-5 • 0-88784-774-9

Atonement
Gaétan Soucy
978-0-88784-780-6 • 0-88784-780-3

The Immaculate Conception
Gaétan Soucy
978-0-88784-783-7 • 0-88784-783-8

The Little Girl Who Was Too Fond of Matches
Gaétan Soucy
978-0-88784-781-3 • 0-88784-781-1

Vaudeville!
Gaétan Soucy
978-0-88784-782-0 • 0-88784-782-X

Returning to Earth
Jim Harrison
978-0-88784-786-8 • 0-88784-786-2

True North
Jim Harrison
978-0-88784-729-5 • 0-88784-729-3

De Niro's Game
Rawi Hage
978-0-88784-813-1 • 0-88784-813-3

Paradise
A. L. Kennedy
978-0-88784-738-7 • 0-88784-738-2

The Big Why
Michael Winter
978-0-88784-734-9 • 0-88784-734-X